Best regards
Mia Capley

AN ELIZABETH'S PLACE MYSTERY

MIA CAPLEY

TWISTS OF TIME

Stratton Press, LLC
1603 Capitol Ave, Suite 310,
Cheyenne, WY 82001
www.stratton-press.com
1-888-323-7009

ISBN (Paperback): 978-1-64345-054-4
ISBN (Ebook): 978-1-64345-260-9

Printed in the United States of America

This book is dedicated to Hunter, Caitlin, and Will. No matter how surreal the world may seem, you are always my rocks that keep me steady! I love you!

Acknowledgments

There is never a time when an author walks alone. There are always those special folks who keep you on track and encourage you without whom a book would never see a printing date. To those who have been my cheerleaders, I sincerely thank you.

My late father, James W. Atwood, read every word of each novel before painting the front covers. He saw my vision and created my heart on canvas. This book stands in remembrance fo him.

And to my precious husband, Micky, thank you for your love that gives flight to my imaging.

Philippians 1:3

Other books by Mia Capley

One More Time, an Elizabeth's Place mystery
My Magic Carpet Ride, children's book
and coming soon, *Hands of Time*,
an Elizabeth's Place mystery

Chapter 1

'Come on, girl, you can make it,' Ashton Grayson encouraged the old car as it puttered and sputtered down the lonesome road. His gas needle read empty, and his motor sounded shattered as he crossed his fingers, said a little prayer for wings of angels to carry him, and pushed further on the gas pedal.

'Just a little farther, and surely there will be a store or a gas station. Come on…I know we can make it just a bit farther, and I really don't feel like walking with it getting dark in the middle of Nowhere, USA.'

The car made it around a curve in the bumpy road before it shuddered quite determinedly and came to a slow fading sigh. With thought akin to panic, Ashton tried to calm his racing pulse as he put the car into park and turned the key off then on with desperate hope.

'Rrrr' was the only sound the car made before it simply ground with several clicks in a very ominous way.

'Drat!' He screamed at no one in particular as he once again tried to get the car to start. 'It's getting dark, ole girl, and we've been together for too many miles for you to bail on me now. Come on, come on…'

With a growl of frustration, Ashton slowly turned the ignition, hoping for a miracle.

A miracle was what he got! The car, made in the early 1990s, came to life with grand sputter, hesitated, and purred with what little life was left in the poor old thing.

Ashton and Red Belle, as he dubbed her, had started a trip together several months ago with no map or direction. They simply drove. Beginning in the far corner of Colorado where his last job as an analysis had come to a screeching halt, they had travelled the country. They'd taken small breaks along the way, like the time he had to replace her water pump, and they'd stayed in certain areas because they were attached for a brief time, like when he had to have all four tyres and the alternator replaced. But mainly, they tootled along with no destination in sight.

For those moments, the wayfaring voyage life had suited them, but as the days on the calendar that laid on the front passenger seat were crossed out, Ashton knew it was time to quit running and find a place to settle—if only for a while. In other words, a short while to either fix Red Belle or, heaven prevent it, replace her with a new vehicle.

'Okay, just keep it up, slow and steady,' he encouraged the car. 'There's gotta be something out here soon.'

Going at a crawl slower than a snail's pace, the car lights finally beamed on a stop sign, rusty with age.

'Civilisation!' he cheered. 'Surely a stop sign, albeit old, is a sign of civilisation, right?'

Looking both directions but never fully coming to a complete stop, Ashton and Red Belle crossed the road and headed on down the way. He knew that if there was any traffic official anywhere around, his missed stop sign should garner attention. But even that wasn't in his favour!

Lights blinked in the distance, and Aston's first ray of hope sprung to life. Red Belle seemed to sense company as well and decided then and there to simply die. So she did.

'Oh, gosh, please, please start again.' Ashton threw the gear shift into park and waited a moment before cranking the engine. Even before he did, he had the horrible feeling she wouldn't start.

Suddenly from under the hood came a *bang*! Through the tepid darkness, white clouds of hissing steam and smoke came rolling into the night air. Ashton knew his boat was sunk, and only a tow truck would move Red Belle any farther down the road.

With his head on the steering wheel and his heart racing at a thundering pace, he debated between getting out of the car that he felt wasn't a bright idea on a dark road, or staying in the car that also didn't sound reasonable considering the spewing sounds coming from the hood. Reluctantly, he opted for the first idea and unbuckled his seat belt as he once again spotted twinkling lights coming his way down the road.

He unlocked the car door and took the keys from the ignition in one swift move as he opened and climbed out of Red Belle. Why he took the keys he would later reflect on with consternation since there was no way anyone could have started the car and driven it away from where she sat. But as was his nature, he carefully stowed them in his pocket and reached back inside the car to turn the hazard lights on for passers-by.

The vehicle coming towards him sounded as bad as Red Belle obviously felt for it squeaked and squealed as it made its way around a curve and bounced through a pothole. The truck was not rolling with much more speed than he had been capable of, so he wondered if perhaps some magnetic force in this area of the world gave moving vehicles some sort of hex so that they didn't function properly. If that was the case, maybe there wasn't anything at all wrong with his car, and he just needed to leave—like yesterday before he'd even arrived!

Slamming the door shut and moving to the trunk of the car, he ran his hands through his sandy hair. His mother said whenever he was upset about something, the first thing to be attacked was his hair. Tonight was no different as it stood in chaotic disarray. Shoving his hands in his pockets, he leaned against the trunk and waited for the oncoming traffic to sweep past him before he opened the boot to see if anything inside could help him start the car.

Slowly the squeaking came to a stop—a sliding stop, but a stop. How anyone could slide to a stop when the automobile was only traveling at ten miles an hour, he wondered.

The driver of the truck rolled down the window a small fraction and, between the door frame and the window glass, stuck her nose out into the air. He knew immediately it was a female driver because her sweet smell floated towards him on the night breeze. Slowly, as to not alarm her, he turned in her direction with a raised hand.

'Hi, ma'am,' he greeted, still standing against his car. He waited for her to respond before he ventured further in conversation.

'Hi,' said a soft but firm voice. 'Having car troubles, are you?'

He couldn't make out any of her features, but Ashton decided she sounded nice enough to approach with a slow pace. 'I am, and the worst of it is that I don't know where I am or where I should go to find any help. Could you…?'

The truck door came open, and a petite young woman slid from the seat and to the ground. Sizing him up, she hung onto the door frame as she asked how it sounded before it quit.

'If I move my truck so the lights shine onto your car, do you think we could fix it enough to get it down the road to the store?'

'I really don't think there is any hope for her'—he grimaced—'but you're welcome to try if you don't mind.'

'Sure thing,' she said. 'You're not from around here, huh?' She once again pulled herself into the cab. 'I remember how being the new kid felt and neighbours help neighbours. I'll give it a whirl.'

For the first time in several very long minutes, Ashton felt a tiny spark of optimism light. He went back to the car door, opened it, and felt for the hood latch on the left side of the steering wheel. Popping it, he watched her pull the truck forward with the lights shining just right to let them see under the hood.

'Have you had the car long?' she asked as she walked up to him. 'Better yet, do you know how to fix it?'

He chuckled and actually felt light-hearted in doing so. 'I've had this car so long that if she's really done for, I think I will personally bury her.'

She grinned up at him, and he suddenly felt as if her smile had kicked him in the chest. She was not only an angel come to rescue his stranded status, she was sheer charm and delight! What a smile!

'Okay, if you hit this thingamajig with a hammer or tap this box thing with a screwdriver, sometimes my truck will start again. Want to try that?'

With his eyes wide, he stood there staring at her, not knowing what to say.

'Well, do you want to try, or is there something else that might work better?'

Ashton quickly retreated to the trunk and, carrying a wrench and a small ball-peen hammer, he handed them to her and jumped behind the wheel. 'Tell me when to try to start Red Belle,' he said out the crack in the door just as the wrench clanged against something and the hammer clunked against something else.

'Try it!' she said, standing back from the still-steaming engine.

Turning the key, the engine just made a clinking noise, but nothing more.

Clunk! Ping! The sounds flew again. Ashton once again turned the key and heard a clicking that rose to a whiz.

Clunk! Ping! came the sound again.

'Now pump the gas pedal just a little!' she shouted.

Ashton did as he was told and turned the key.

Rrr went the motor as a 'yippee' uttered from Ashton's breath as the car came to life sluggishly.

Keeping his foot slightly on the accelerator, he gave her a thumbs up out the door.

'You're not gonna get far on this motor,' the spry lady said as she wiped her hands on her jeans and walked up to him. 'You're not going anywhere tonight, that's for sure.'

'Do you think I could get to a motel and then have her towed to a station in the morning?'

'Well, if we had a motel around here, maybe, but we don't. So I'll follow you as you drive just up this road to the store. In the morning, I'll call Emmett and see if he can come tow you to his garage.'

'You're a lifesaver! Ashton said. 'That would be great, if you don't mind. I mean, you were just coming from that direction, so I hope I'm not keeping you from your family.'

'Oh, they'll be all right for another minute or two, and the car will be safe at the store. We don't have a great many strange cars around, so I'll make a few calls so no one is worried. Let me back up, and we'll start on our way.'

And before Ashton could say another word, she was in the truck, and it was in gear headed backwards for a distance before the lights left his car and the truck turned in the road. Keeping a steady foot and as calm a mind as he could, Ashton followed his rescuer down the road and onto a highway.

Within just a few yards, the truck pulled into a paved parking lot, and Ashton followed suit, pulling over to the far side of the building so as not to be in anyone's way. Before he could turn off the engine, she was out of the truck and motioning for him to roll down his window.

'Before you turn it off, pull out, back up, and then back up to the store. Emmett is getting a bit elderly, and having it ready to just be towed away will be a big help for him.'

Ashton did as he was told while she stood and watched. He noticed her take a notepad from her shirt pocket and a pen from behind her ear as he placed the car in park. Scribbling a note, she tore the page from the book and stuffed it in the corner of the store's door. Undoubtedly, she was letting the store's owner know that Red Belle belonged to him and that Emmett, whoever he was, would be coming to get her in the morning.

'Okay, get your stuff and get into my truck,' she said, a bit demandingly, as she approached his car. 'We don't have a motel for over twenty miles, and you can't sleep in the ditch, so as long as you promise that you aren't a murderer, you can stay at my house.'

'I'm sorry?' Ashton couldn't believe his ears. 'What? You want a complete stranger to come stay at your house? Ma'am, you don't know me and—'

'I can solve that problem,' she said, sticking out her hand. 'My name is Sara McKenzie. Nice to meet you, Mr…?'

'Grayson,' he said. 'Aston Grayson. If you're sure you don't mind, it would be a real relief to have somewhere to sleep, but I can stay on the back seat of the car.'

She glanced in the car window and laughed out loud. 'Somehow I think that would not only be uncomfortable for a man of your height, but I also think it would be a little lumpy considering all the stuff already on that seat. Where's your suitcase or whatever you need. Let's go.'

So with his arms loaded and her arms full, they loaded the truck and started back the way they had just come from.

'Have you lived here long?' he asked as they drove. 'What I saw before it got dark was really pretty land.'

'No, I inherited this land over a year ago. My father owned it, and when he passed, I got it. So I left the city and couldn't resist staying on here once I arrived.'

'So you moved your family here.'

'Yes, Oscar, Petrie, and I live here with Thunder and Breeze. We have lots of guests who visit from time to time. Some of them can be very interesting.'

Sara smiled as she turned into a gravel driveway. The lane had trees on both sides as the lights from the truck bounced off them. Large magnolias seemed to extend a hand of greeting as they rounded a curve. Wrought iron gates greeted them, and a stand of holly trees welcomed them into the front garden.

As the lights hit the house, it seemed to stand straighter and glow. It was simply incredible to see as tall turrets reached for the sky and gleaming windows winked at their approach.

'Mr Grayson, I hope you're not afraid of the dark for dark it is here, and I hope you will enjoy your stay with me. Welcome to Elizabeth's Place.'

Chapter 2

Sara McKenzie inwardly wondered at the person she'd become in the last year or so. It was amazing to hear herself invite this total stranger into her house. Not because she wasn't hospitable, but because she would never have stopped for a lone stranger on the road much less brought him home a mere year ago. How things had changed.

As the two wearying bodies gathered Ashton's belongings from the truck, Sara skimmed through the year just past. Her father had died and left her this farm a million miles from where she'd called home. She acted very independently and hopped a plane to this wonderful world that seemed hidden away from modern-day chaos and busy-ness. The minute she'd opened the doors of the house, she'd realised that she was truly at home here.

Finding out the name of the home was Elizabeth's Place, she'd researched the history, battled ghosts, upset land invaders, and befriended a treasure trove of local folks who were now her family. And she'd met and developed deep, deep feelings for William, the house's ghost. Now, she embraced each day to its fullest and lovingly rejoiced that God and her father, the late Rhett McKenzie, had deemed this to be her farm, her heart.

'Here let me get that big bag,' said Ashton as he heaved a duffel bag onto his shoulder while he carried a large suitcase through the screen door. 'Wow! This is like stepping back in time. How'd you manage to find a place like this?' Ashton took in his surroundings as the wide entryway gave way to a large curving staircase and wide doors opening into other rooms. 'This is a dream work!'

'Thank you very much,' Sara replied, shutting the thick wooden front door against the night chill. 'The house was a gift from my late father. He had somehow come across it and kept it for me. He was always looking out for me!'

Though Sara's face bore a grin, the sound of the words coming from her mouth gave credit to the loss she still felt when she returned home from trail riding and found her father was dead. The house was sometimes a bittersweet gift.

'Well, just put your stuff down here for now, and I'll go see what I can find for us to eat. Are you hungry?'

'Starved and so thirsty,' Ashton replied. 'What can I help you with?'

'Let's just see where the kitchen stands on the pantry level, and then we'll take it from there,' said Sara as she led him into the wide kitchen that was comprised of new, modern equipment where he'd expected to see a potbellied stove or a pump instead of running water.

'Well, you surprised me again, Sara McKenzie. I must say that sometimes my imagination can get the best of me.'

She chuckled at his astonishment, and it was the most cheerful sound he'd heard in a long time.

'So, what do you like?' she asked, pulling open the refrigerator door and staring inside. 'Would you like some baked chicken and potatoes, or are you more of a sandwich kinda guy?'

'I will eat anything that doesn't eat me first,' he quipped in return, his smile spreading from ear to ear. 'Is the chicken already baked, or will you have to cook it? If you do, then don't, and I will happily eat a sandwich…something simple.'

'Sandwich it is, then!' Sara reached for the fixings and grabbed a loaf of bread from the cabinet. 'Do you like cheese and tomato with your ham sandwich? You do eat ham, don't you? If not, there is always baloney.'

'Not being a man who ever passes up new experiences, I'll try the baloney, but I may also eat the ham if that's all right. And yes, cheese and tomato is wonderful even by itself.'

She pointed out the cabinet with the glasses and plates, rounded up some lettuce and pickles, and then, with everything on the table, grabbed two soft drinks and some ice.

'Dig in,' she told him. 'I don't stand on formality when I'm by myself so often, but I do need to check on Oscar and Petrie. Be right back.'

Though he raised his dark brows in question, Ashton said not a word and instead focused on the food. When he heard tiny yipping and clicking on the hardwood floors, he laughed in relief that her companions were canine in type, not humans at all. Why this was such a relief to him, he didn't understand.

The clicking ceased at the edge of the kitchen door, and a muffled low growling sound spread through the room.

'Sorry,' Sara said hastily as she picked up a Yorkshire terrier and a tiny red Dachshund. 'This is Petrie.' She lifted the Yorkie higher in the air. 'And this is Oscar. They're rather protective at times. We're the Three Musketeers. We've been together for… gosh, I can't even remember how long. Lots of years and many storms at any rate!'

With the dogs still sniffing Ashton's pants leg, Sara washed her hands and scrubbed away the motor dirt that remained there. Then she pulled out a chair and plopped into it with anything but social grace.

'So where did you move from when you came here?' Ashton took a big bite of a sandwich and then grabbed a pickle. 'You don't seem like a country girl to me.'

'I am anything but…well, I *was* anything but a country girl, but God has a way of fitting square pegs into round holes.' Sara laughed. 'My father and mother were both business success stories, and though I lived with them and mostly saw them at nightly meals, they did travel a lot. I attended a private school and even had finishing lessons with the emphasis in etiquette, so please don't tell anyone you ate a sandwich for dinner or that I served you in the kitchen.'

Ashton was reluctant to laugh until her smile forced on from him. 'I think I know what you mean about private schools and social responsibilities,' he said. 'Though my parents were much less concerned about social graces in my case. I grew up along the West Coast, and things are not quite so strict these days. I promise not to tell your secret, but I don't think it would be too bad if I told someone.'

'Oh, you mustn't!' she cried. 'Somehow, Mrs Cummings would somehow find out and rap my knuckles for breaking so many rules. My back is presently touching the back of the chair, and I didn't lay the table as a respectable young woman should.'

Ashton laughed so hard that he choked on a bite and found himself with tears streaming down his face from the force of the hilarity that resulted from her total look of fright. She had to be joking!

'Honest to Pete!' she exclaimed, clambering from her chair and thumping him on the back. 'Are you okay?'

Wrestling with his laughter to get it under control and aspiring to breathe normally, Ashton could only raise his arms and reach for her shoulder to reassure her he was in no danger.

'You are so funny, Sara!' he finally was able to say. 'I haven't laughed this much in years!'

'Is that why you are driving way out here in the sticks? A need to laugh?'

'You're darn tooting, it is!' he replied, wiping mustard from his cheeks and trying not to laugh aloud again. 'It has been a lot of years since I just took life in stride,' he said. 'I was an analyst at a software company in Oregon, but the pressure to produce and then sell was brutalising. I went to work early and was about the last one to leave, if we left, and the hours were driving me nuts. I really never planned to work in the field, but the money was great, and the experience was something I could build on eventually. Or so I thought at one time. Now, I don't know.

'Don't get me wrong. I was very good at the job I did, and my bank balance reflects it, but if you work all the time, you never seem to have time to enjoy life. Kinda a 'twist of time,' I guess.'

'I'm sure my parents must have felt much the same way,' Sara said in reflection. 'Daddy was always developing new ideas and competing with some other company to stay on top. The last few years it was just the two of us after Mom died, but she had been a dedicated worker too.'

'And what do you like to do?'

The question just stood on still air for a time before she answered.

'Well, if you'd asked me a few years ago where my path was leading, I might have told you something to do with the arts—sketching, drawing, designing.

But now, I think, I would say that I was born to be a farmer!'

'Really? A farmer? Like plow fields and grow crops and hay and stuff? Really?'

'Yeah, I think so. I really haven't tried, though I did have a successful garden this summer. I think that with the help of my friends, I could eventually make Elizabeth's Place into a thriving farm again.'

'I must say that I've never experienced such an amazing outlook from a city girl cum country queen. Well, unless you count reruns of *Green Acres* on TV Land!'

Sara considered herself as a possible modern-day Oliver Wendell Douglas, the main character in the 1960s sitcom about a New York attorney who decides to move to the country and grow crops.

She laughed aloud at the thought of herself in such a role.

'I guess that could be me in a way. Maybe my dreams are as silly as the actors made Oliver's to be, but…Well, at least I don't have Zsa Zsa Gabor playing my sidekick!'

The tinkling of their laughter continued into the night. Two strangers on a dark country road becoming quick friends was almost as funny as an episode of the old television show. When they finally rose from the table and cleared away the sandwich clutter, they were both ready for a good night's sleep.

'Let's get your luggage and stuff, and I'll show you your room,' Sara said as she masked a yawn. 'The sun comes up early, but I don't necessarily rise with it, so you can feel free to sleep in tomorrow. When you're ready, I'll take you to Emmett's and see what he can do for your car. Why do you keep it if you have so much trouble with it?'

'Like you, there is sentimental attachment to Red Belle,' he explained as they climbed the stairs. 'She belonged originally to my grandfather, and when I turned sixteen, she became mine. I could have bought something new long ago, but she's kinda like a friend.'

Nodding her head in understanding, Sara took him into the room at the right-hand corner of the second floor. The door was already opened when they approached it, and the sight of the half tester bed almost took his breath away.

'Isn't this something!' Ashton exclaimed. 'I feel like I've landed at Tara!'

'Not quite Tara, but Elizabeth's Place was the pride of this area in her day. There is a bath just down the hall this way, and towels and such are in the closet. Help yourself, and if you can't find what you need, give me a shout. I'm at the other end of the hall.'

'Sara, thank you so much for your hospitality,' Ashton said as he ruffled his hair with his hands. At over six feet tall, the motion made him look like a giant's child. 'I don't really know how to thank you.'

'Say good night, and that will be thanks enough. Hope you sleep well. There are extra blankets in the chest at the foot of the bed. Good night!'

'Night, Sara, sleep well.'

Sara was almost to her doorway when his last words reached her ears. She yawned and stretched, bending down to scoop up her dogs.

Unbidden the verse about doing unto others swam through her mind. Maybe she had been rash to ask a stranger into her home, but who knew. She might just be entertaining an angel. Or being hoodwinked by the devil himself!

Chapter 3

It was almost eight o'clock before Sara felt brave enough to call Herb Carblo, owner of the little store down the way to let him know why there was a broken-down car sitting in his parking lot. She took a deep breath as the phone rang and rang and rang.

Feelings changed from anxious to anticipation to worry in a short beat of her heart when the ringing continued. Finally, the click of the receiver as it was lifted quieted the ringing but not her concern.

'Good morning, Carblo—'

'Marian, is everything all right? This is Sara, and—'

'I know who you are, sweetie, and nothing is wrong. I am just standing on my head trying to clean the cooler, and Dad can't seem to hear the phone ringing on and on.' It was obvious that Marian, Herb's daughter, was perplexed as she continued to say, not necessarily to Sara or into the phone, 'or he's just too stubborn this morning to bother to answer! Now, what can I do for you, dear?'

Marian was twenty-plus years older than Sara, but the two of them often visited like sisters of the same age instead of nearly a generation apart. Sara could hear the exasperation in Marian's voice and the breathing that accompanied it only accentuated both her frustration with her elderly father and her standing on her head in the cooler to clean the shelves.

'Oh, I'm so glad everything is okay. I was just worried when the phone kept ringing. That's not like Herb. What's his problem today?'

'Seems that someone, I won't say who, left an old car in the parking lot and a note in his door here at the store. It's not that he minds the car being left. It was that the note disturbed him. He's been in a state, I'll tell ya!'

'May I speak with him, please? Maybe I can get him back to rights. I'm sorry I upset him so and made your day rough!'

'Don't bother me none, you know that, but I just wondered how you got tangled up with the car. Was it abandoned? Did you get hijacked?'

Sara rolled her eyes as the questions continued. She was savvy enough to know the questions were rhetorical and that it was part of her punishment for being shortsighted in the Carblos' eyes.

'I'm ready to take my medicine, Marian. Just hand him the phone.'

'Alrighty then, if you're sure…'

'Hello!' came the stern grunt of a greeting when Herb finally took the phone.

'Herb, I'm sorry about the car and about scaring you.'

'You didn't scare me, missy. What you do is your concern after all, but I'd think you'd have better sense than to just go off with some stranger and leave me a note in the door. You could have called me to let me know.'

'Yes sir,' she muttered, knowing in his eyes she would always be a newborn cub. 'The man is very nice, and I couldn't exactly leave him to sleep on the street, could I? Anyway, I've called Emmett's this morning, and he is coming to get the car to see if it will ever run again.'

'He's already been here and picked up that piece of junk,' Herb said. 'Now, where's this boy, and what does he have to say for himself?'

'He's in the shower, and I don't know what you mean, but he is from out of town, I don't know his parents or his lineage, and no, he didn't try anything during the night. But thanks for being concerned. I'll see you shortly!'

Sara didn't wait for Herb to say anything but hung up the phone and went to the bottom of the stairs. She couldn't hear the water running, so she yelled up the stairs for Ashton to dress quickly and to insulate his hide well because it was time to go see the general!

* * *

With a feather duster sticking out from his back pocket, Herb Carblo settled into his normal spot at the table of the store. His ladder-back chair had been in use for so many years that the sag in the seat molded to his body perfectly. Not that Herb was a large man; quite the opposite was true of the tall and lanky eighty-some-year-old who, along with his late wife Miss Irma, had started the store from scratch just after they married. Ms Irma had informed Herb that she wanted her husband to be an upstanding gentleman who worked hard. She would be the wife waiting at the end of the day.

Thinking to himself that he could put her to work and only work half as hard as she wanted him to, he decided to open a store. Little did he know that working for Ms Irma was harder than any day working on the road crew! He's dusted, swept, and mopped more floors and shelves than more janitors would in a lifetime. Ms Irma didn't like dust or mud or dirt of any kind, and if someone tracked in the teeniest bit of something akin to it, Herb was the one who cleaned it up under her watchful eye while she tended to the customers with smiles and tinkling laughter.

Oh! How he missed Ms Irma!

Marian was the spitting image of her mother but took gumption after her father. She'd rather talk a blue streak than even dust a can on the shelf. Therefore, the cans had to be wiped down as a customer bought one, and the feather duster was a permanent fixture in Herb's back pocket.

Herb glanced at the clock that hung over the entryway of the store, the hands telling him to expect Ross and Lem at any time. As soon as the clock hands hit 10.30, the two men, friends of his since his elementary school days, would be rolling in to get up the energy to order lunch.

Their days varied very little this late in life. They were thrilled to still be independent enough to drive and keep house for themselves. All the wives were gone now; children were sparse and far away for Lem and Ross. Marian of course lived with Herb since her husband died some twelve years ago.

Herb reared back in the chair, balancing on the two back legs. This was a small pleasure that he both afforded himself and had a certain pride in doing it. How many folks his age could balance on their two legs much less balance a chair that way!

'Howdy, friend!' Ross Barnett said as he whistled his way in the door. Ross was one of a kind in Herb's opinion. From the day Ross learned how to whistle as a seven-year-old, he'd never gone a day without whistling. Of course, part of that was that there was this space between his teeth that let air escape when he talked or sang or hummed. But he never failed to whistle a tune, recognisable or not, when he walked across the floor or across a field.

Ross had spent his working years as the manager of a factory in Gladesville. But it had shut down about thirty years ago, and nothing had taken its place, so Ross had retired to try his hand at farming. That project lasted just under a year when he'd had a heart attack. His wife Irene looked after him like a mother bird until she passed away of sheer worrisome-ness three years ago. Now, Ross spent his days whistling and visiting the sick and shut-ins, but mostly just stayed at the store with Herb, Marian, and Lem.

He folded his lean limbs into 'his' chair around the table and smiled in relaxation. 'Hey ya, hey ya,' Herb said as Ross settled into his spot. 'What's up this morning?'

'Same as always, I 'spect,' Ross said. 'Seen Lem this morning?'

'Not time fer him yet,' Herb said sharply. 'Look at the time. He's still lallygagging about, I 'magin. Why? What's up?'

'Oh, notin' much. Old Man Lemmons had some cattle out in the road early this morning, and I wondered if he knew about 'em. You know sometimes they get over on Lem's place and make a mess of everything. Figured Lem would've called if they were there.'

'Ain't heard nothing from him, not yet anyways. He get 'em back in?'

'I don't know. They were in the road when I went to the doctor's office this morning. Had to have my blood sugar checked, ya know. But when I came back, I didn't see 'em, and I wasn't gonna call him. He'd have recruited me to go find 'em.'

Herb nodded his head in agreement and stood, pulling up his pants as he did. 'Want a Coke?' he asked, but before Ross could answer, he slid the glass top across a cooler and took out three by the neck and placed them on the table. A bottle opener hung beside the cooler, and though the drinks now had twist-off tops, Herb still liked to pull them off with the opener.

The bell above the door tinkled as Herb shuffled back to his seat. Expecting Lem, he never turned around but set the soft drinks on the table in front of Ross and sat back down.

Lem never missed a beat. He crossed the floor with his staggered way of walking and plopped into a chair like many would toss a can in the trash. The chair rocked back and forth as his stubby legs flew in the air, but no one got excited as this was the way Lem always sat down. One day the chair was going to refuse to hold his exaggerated seating method, but for now…well, Lem had always been a lucky one!

Each with a drink in his hand, the store was quiet. Marian was cleaning out coolers and bins because the milkman was expected later on this week, and she wanted it clean. If the milkman came, then generally the grocery and sundries' man wasn't far behind.

Since the store did a minimum of business, Marian had stopped worrying about making an order from either of them. She just let them fill as they founded necessary and sold whatever they brought little by little to those who stopped to shop.

The men were mumbling about the weather and a chance of thunderstorms when the door's bell tinkled again. Herb stopped what he was saying and watched the lovely young lady saunter her way in the store. In his mind, Sara was the closest family he had next to Marian, and he was about to have a say with her about her rashness when he saw the offender walking behind her towards the table.

'Good morning, fellas,' she said with a smile that spread across her face. Herb thought that smile brightened a dark room. He was so fond of her. 'See you're already hitting the bottles this morning.'

As she laughed, the world chimed with the melody, and all thoughts of fussing over her sorted behavior last night flew out of Herb's head. Instead, he extended his arm around her waist and motioned for her to sit down with them.

As she managed a chair or two away from the wall where the extras stood, Sara introduced each man to Ashton.

'Nice to meet all of you,' the young scalawag said, shaking each hand in turn. 'Sara has told me a lot about you gentlemen in the last few hours. I feel like I know you too.'

'Well, ya don't!' Herb said. 'And you don't know her either, so don't go getting' all familiar with her!'

Sara laughed and patted him on the shoulder, although she was a bit taken aback by his tone of voice. 'It's okay, Herb, I promise that Ashton is the perfect gentleman. So, have you heard anything about his car from Emmett?'

'Naw, I hadn't. Don't guess Emmett feels it's any of my business about his car.'

'Hi, Marian,' Sara said when she saw her round the shelving and head towards the counter.

'Hey there, Sara,' Marian replied cheerfully. 'Who's your new friend there?'

'This is Ashton Grayson. Ashton, this is Herb's daughter, Marian Sanders. I think you know almost the whole community now.'

Crawdad was a tiny place in the road that most missed as they drove between Gladesville and Traceland, neither big metropolis themselves. The site of many Civil War battles and troop maneuvers during the late 1800s, Crawdad was known for its beautiful hills. Many folks might stop to look at the mountain range in the distances, but few settled down in the country air long enough for the town to grow into anything but an 'unincorporated' community. There was no post office, no bank, and no grocery store save the Carblo Grocery owned by Herb Carblo. In fact, the community seat was the store's table area as well as the communication hub of the area.

'Anyone hungry?' Marian asked as she wiped her hands with a paper towel. 'Bread's fresh today, and I've got a wonderfully ripe tomato that is just begging to be sliced!'

Hands all around the table rose to volunteer to eat. Marian chuckled as she pulled out chicken salad for Lem, pimento cheese for Ross, and ham for her father. 'What about you two?' she asked, looking at Sara and Ashton.

'Is it possible to have a tomato sandwich, ma'am?' Ashton asked with an eyebrow raised. 'My grandmother used to slice cucumbers and tomatoes and put them on fresh bread. That was the best sandwich in the world!'

Marian smiled at the young man with real pleasure, a sign she approved of him.

'As a matter of fact, that is one of Sara's favourites. Mine too. One 'mater sandwich coming up! Sara, want the same?'

But Sara was already out of her seat and out the front door as two black bulls stood nose to nose in the parking lot.

'Hey!' she screamed at them as she ran out the door. 'Hey! Shoo! Get away from here!'

Both bulls turned and looked at the woman as if she was a nut before swinging heads at each other and bellowing into the air. As the bulls turned to bite and nip at each other, one reared up on two legs and came at the other.

Standing close enough to feel their heat, Sara stumbled as she stepped back to get out of their way.

'Enough of that!' Ashton said as he pushed at the massive animals, whose tempers with each other were getting out of control. Dodging a hind leg that kicked in his direction, Ashton sidestepped into a manure pile, skidded, and slid right into Sara, knocking her between the front hooves of the bulls. As they again launched at each other, a gunshot rang in the air, and both turned at a running pace to escape the sound.

Sara lay on the ground, waiting to see what the outcome was. Gradually she sat up and looked around her. There stood Herb with his rifle in the crook of his arm, Marian with the dish towel twisted in her hands, and Lem and Ross laughing from the doorway. Herb just grinned and offered her a hand up from the ground, stepping in and splashing more of the muck on Ashton as he did.

Chapter 4

Even though the day had had its bumps and tumbles, by the time the sun set in Crawdad, Herb and Ashton were becoming quick friends, and Lem and Ross, as well as Marian, had already taken a liking to the personable young man.

The five of them had journeyed to Emmett's Garage after some cleaning to check out the car's prognosis. However, the report wasn't a good one.

'Well, your pistons are shot for one thing, and your radiator is about to go.' Emmett began. Rather a squirrelly man, Emmett did one thing in his life, and he did it well: mechanic work. It was said he could fix a box of parts and turn them into a well-oiled machine, though Sara had no first-hand experience with that.

'But is there any way to fix what is wrong with her?' Ashton asked anxiously.

'Son, that's the problem. Don't seem to be nothin' wrong with the car. It just won't run.'

'But, Emmett, what is wrong with the car so that it don't run?' Herb asked, losing his patience for all this high drama Emmett was trying to sell the boy.

'I don't know,' the grouchy man said. 'I told you there are things that could be changed but nothing that is actually keeping the car from running properly. I think the car was overheating from the steam you said you saw, but the water levels are okay, and the other checks I've done were right as rain as well. Just let it rest a day or two with me. I'll keep checkin' her out and see if I can see somethin'. Don't worry, I won't rob you. I'm just as curious to see what the problem is as you are. When are you planning on leaving town?'

Ashton looked to Sara and then to Herb without answering. 'I can wait as long as you say, as long as Sara doesn't tell me to leave,' Ashton said with what could have passed for a tiny smile. 'I don't want to inconvenience anyone.'

Herb thumped Ashton on the back and looked to Sara. 'You okay with him being around a few more days? If not, he can stay with Lem or Ross. They both got extra rooms.'

The other two men looked at each other as if to ask who gave Herb control over their spare bedrooms, but they said nothing to go against his words.

Sara smiled at Herb then turned to Emmett. 'Whenever you say the car is fit enough to drive, I'll bring him back to see you. In the meantime, I should probably get all these fellas back to the store before

Marian comes hunting for us. Thank you, Emmett. I trust you, so I know that Ashton here does too!'

With a wink to her, Ashton opened the door and ushered them all out of the garage. As they trooped out, Emmett was heard to mutter, 'Don't know what's wrong with this dang car. Must be gremlins inside or ghosts pulling the wires. Just ain't right about it. Something just ain't right.'

If only he'd known how true his words were.

He sat in the loft of the barn and waited for her to come with the evening feedings. He knew her every move and that she would have special treats for all the wildlife in the barn's vicinity. She would feel the squirrels, the birds, the possums, and the raccoon as well as the old owl who lived in the rafters, and the even the smelly skunk that inhabited the hole in the floor just to the right of the last stall wall. She would be there for hours talking to the horses and cleaning the old leather workings that she attempted to bring back to life with each stroke.

Then he knew she would head outside to the pasture where she'd walk and sing. She left dog food in places the foxes could find and look for signs that any more damage had been done to the property, such as the cave explosions that had occurred only a few short months ago. They had been man-made of course by a group of men who thought they could find scads of gold and treasures if they blew up the area. Too bad for them they never checked a map to see which cave the gold might have been hidden in long ago.

He had stood beside her through all those terrifying days. He'd watched over her from every angle the farm had, and still today, he continued to guard her.

There was no doubt in his mind that he loved her. Not with the depth that his love abounded for Elizabeth, but he knew he loved her. And in her way, Sara loved him too. There was just that one small problem that kept them apart, but even that never completely separated them.

In the dark hours of the night, he would find her sitting in the music room where she admitted she hoped he would look for her. And then he would play first the violin and the harp and finally the piano for her. His heart was in every note. She was in his every thought.

If only their paths had crossed at a different time in life, maybe their love for each other could have become a reality. But there were years between them, and they were, in effect, worlds apart. But she knew his secrets, and he knew many of hers. They had both experienced the harsh pain of a loved one's passing.

His precious wife Elizabeth had died under the full moon in the pasture just outside the barn, although he still didn't understand what compelled her to ride her horse that night. Whatever or whoever it was had taken her from his life with her.

He'd been astonished when he'd first seen Sara. She had Elizabeth's beautiful eyes and charming smile. Her long hair looked as silky as Elizabeth's was to the touch. And her spunk? Well, she was as feisty as he remembered Elizabeth.

These were the special and memorable things about Elizabeth that drew him to Sara. He'd promised her and himself that he would stay near her forever. And since it didn't appear he was in a hurry to go anywhere, so he would!

If only there wasn't that one thing between them that made them so different, he would scoop her up and carry her away from the world. But there was a major difference. She was so full of life, and he was, well…dead.

Chapter 5

The following day's weather held rain in the forecast, but the morning made light of that prediction and beamed with eye-opening sun. Sara hurried to the barn to take care of Breeze, her large bay gelding, and Storm, a feisty thoroughbred stallion. Both were easily cared for by the petite girl simply because she knew their temperaments as well as her own.

She whistled and hummed as she cleaned stalls. The horses were turned out into the pasture to run a bit while she manned the feeding and watering chores.

Just as she was laying feed for the old opossum in the loft, Ashton yelled from the floor below. 'You in here, Sara? I've been searching for you. I made some coffee and brought you some.'

'I'm up here,' Sara replied as she started down the loft ladder. 'It was time to feed Otis, and I haven't seen him in a couple of days. He's eaten his food I left, but I can't really tell if he's slept here or not.'

'And Otis would be who?'

Sara's bright laugh rang through the barn, chasing the dust bunnies as they floated through the sunlight.

'Otis is a possum, an old and cantankerous thing. He was obviously living in the barn before I came along to disturb him, so as a peace offering, I leave him and the owl kibble to eat. I don't really see either of them, but I know they are here enough to eat treats.'

'You feed the wild animals that live in your barn? On purpose?'

'Of course! All animals have to eat, don't they? Like you. I bet you're ready to eat something, aren't you?'

Ashton leaned against the barn wall and watched as Sara hefted a hay bale from the hallway back into the feed room. He was amazed at her energy and strength that was hidden behind her small body stature and charming personality. In fact, he found himself thinking of her often: how she would feel with her hand tucked into his or how it would feel to see her smile at him the way she did old man Carblo.

He cleared his throat and his mind. 'Hey, Sara, what can I help you with so that you can get finished and come fix breakfast?'

'I am done with these chores, but I would think a bachelor such as you who is independent and a devil-may-care roustabout could come up with his own breakfast. Don't tell me you would rely on little old me to keep you fed!'

Ashton leaned his head and looked at the loft. A tendril of straw floated down as he watched. He realised that Otis was undoubtedly searching for his hidden treats. He laughed.

'Sorry, I didn't mean it to sound like that! I guess I was hoping you would join me for something to eat regardless of whose kitchen we sat in to eat! Forgive me for sounding like an ungrateful house guest and, even more, a male chauvinist!'

He bent his long form over in a bow, his blond hair flitting in his eyes as he did. He casually brushed it aside with one hand while extending the other towards Sara. 'Am I forgiven?'

'Of course,' Sara quipped as she cuffed his head. 'Just don't let it happen again.'

Together the two walked through the barn door, leaving it open to air the dusty air. As they walked slowly through the pasture, Sara took note of the running creek and the field full of wild flowers. Storm and Breeze were enjoying the fresh grazing in the pasture, and even Oscar and Petrie were jumping and playing in the sunlight.

'It's a beautiful day,' Ashton said, raising his face to the sky. 'I can understand why you'd be happy here.'

'Well, it was a change of pace for me when I first arrived,' Sara said. 'I really had it in my head that I would come and visit for a few days—maybe even a couple of weeks—and then put it up for sale and continue with school. For some reason, all thoughts of grad school and the material world faded the minute I stepped out of the rental car. I really felt at home here—I still do. But mostly, I felt that I had come home. It is safe and so quiet and peaceful here that I would be crazy to ever leave.'

They stepped onto the porch and unlaced shoes to leave them on the porch. Instead of heading inside, Sara pulled up the rocking chair on the far side of the porch and invited him to sit. She took the porch step as her seat and pulled her knees up to her chin. He watched her, believing that this was the definition of bliss.

'I could get used to this,' Ashton said as the minutes passed. 'The air is so clear and sweet here.'

'So, what put you on the road in the first place?' Sara turned her face from the direction of the pasture to look at Ashton. His feet were propped on the porch column, and his head was thrown back onto the rocker.

'Oh, several things,' he answered without much enthusiasm for the subject. 'First the job situation like I told you before, but there was the desire to run away and lose myself so that I could find myself. Doesn't that make any sense at all?'

'More than you know. So, what are the plans now that you are truly lost in Crawdad?'

'I don't know really.' Ashton sat forward in the chair and rested his elbows on his knees. He looked over the fields in front of him and internally longed for such as place as this.

'I really hadn't thought I would stop traveling until I met the ocean and couldn't do anything else but turn left or right at the coast. Now, I don't know.

I've had hundreds of miles of thinking and talking out loud and even answering the talking out loud, and I am tired at the moment of driving and talking. Maybe I will find a place somewhere near here to stay for a few months, get to know people instead of myself, and listen to their answers rather than my own.'

'Big decision,' Sara said. 'What do you want to do as a job?'

'Money's not an issue,' he replied as he rose and stretched. 'I have money in the bank both from my savings and from the house I sold when I packed up everything and left. My canvas is completely blank. I can go anywhere and do anything—at least for a while—so I guess I can wing it for a while. Why do you ask?'

'Oh, I was just thinking. I mean, until you get your car running, if you get your car running, you can't really go anywhere, and I could use another set of hands for some things here on the farm. Nothing big, but…'

'You are trying to keep me busy, are you? Well, I will be glad to help you do whatever it is just as soon as you feed me!'

Sara laughed, and he thought it sounded like a ray of sunshine. 'Okay, inside, boy, so I can get you fed before I crack the whip at you!'

He followed her in the house, but not before another set of eyes gazed longingly at her. Sara had warmed William's heart for more than a year, and frankly, he wasn't excited about letting someone else take her away.

Chapter 6

A hint of fall made the evening crisp as Sara pulled a throw around her legs as she sat on the window seat in her room. She closed her journal and clasped her knees to her chest as the moonlight flooded into the room, leaving the deeper sections in dark shadows.

'I know you're here,' she heard herself whisper to him. 'You've been silent for days, but I know you are nearby and watching me.'

The wind blew, making the shutters rattle against the house. When she'd first come to Elizabeth's Place, she'd experienced the feelings of being watched. She knew now that perhaps William had looked after her long before he made his presence known to her and how she had revealed in his nearness since.

William was as much a part of Elizabeth's Place as were the windows. He breathed life into the structure, though he himself had none for William was a ghost.

He had first appeared to her as a kindly neighbour offering assistance, but as the year had progressed, Sara had come to know him as much more. Her only regret of their relationship was that it couldn't be as real as most relationships simply because William had died many, many decades before, yet his spirit had stayed at Elizabeth's Place, a home he had built for his young bride.

When Elizabeth had died in a horse riding accident, his world has silently fallen, much like the tears that had fallen from his eyes as he'd gazed upon her still body that night so long ago. He protected the house, though he hadn't protected his lovely Elizabeth.

Sara had felt his passion and love for his lady. She had felt his pain as he'd told her his story and shared his loss as he'd told her of his failures. And she loved him. Though their love could never be physically shared, Sara loved William with an undying love.

'William, I know you are here. Please, come talk to me.'

She sensed his presence though she couldn't see him. She could almost feel his touch on her hair or a whispery breath against her cheek.

'You've been rather busy of late,' he said into the darkness. 'Your stray puppy seems to be keeping you from me.'

'And this angers you?' she asked, still gazing out the window.

'I've missed your company, to say the least. But I cannot be upset for you seem to be happy with him near. I've heard your laughter, but I am concerned for your welfare. You don't really know this man, and yet he is here in your house.'

'I have you to guard me,' she replied with bravado. 'You've long been my knight in shining armour, so I've always felt safe when you are nearby.'

'Rusty armour perhaps, my dear, but yes, I will always be here to protect you. But you shouldn't push your luck. There may come a time when I can't be near. I would not want to find you in harm's way. Being careful of your actions will keep you safe.'

'Are you jealous?' Sara chuckled at the ridiculousness of this idea. 'What a romantic notion!'

'Jealousy is not an emotion that bides one's time well. But I was perfectly content to be here with you alone. You've brought life back into this house, and I shall never be anything but grateful for that happiness. I only wish I could give you such happiness.'

With longing, William watched her as her eyes grew sleepy. When she rose for her bed, he tucked the covers around her and watched her sleep, listening to the small noises that she made as she drifted into a world of mystery.

'I pray you sweet dreams, my dear,' he whispered, 'for you'll be in mine.'

And dream Sara did. She dreamed of swirling darkness that threatened to take her under an abyss and keep her there. In the pits, she felt despair and agony; she couldn't catch her breath. Looming over her, black clouds whipped across the sky of the pit, and dozens of horned monsters blew icy air around the ever-deepening waves.

As the dreaming Sara floated down long dark hallways, her hands slid across slick rock-covered walls. *Slimy*, she thought to herself as the winds blew her farther from the moonlit opening. *And cold.* She shivered.

Wrapping her arms around herself, she became aware that she had no real control of where she was headed. Her feet never touched the ground. In fact, she could neither see nor reach the ground. Above her, the winged beasts flew just behind her, never reaching her but always there.

In her dream, Sara could try to escape those who, to her thinking, were chasing her, although her speed never increased, and her journey never had a route of escape. The whirling screams and the dizzying noises circled around and around her, tumbling over and over her billowing body as she went on and on, farther and farther down the tunnel.

Where was she? How did she escape?

Fear was suffocating her as she tried to turn backwards, swimming against the raging tides that pulled her under the gigantic emotions that assailed her. There was an invisible force that was shaking her and wailing her name over and over.

'Sara! Sara! You're having a nightmare! Wake up!'

Under the weight that held her in its arms, the terrified girl reached for any help she could gain, never attaining a hold but grasping for the security net just the same.

'Sara! Wake up! Sara!'

Ashton shook her to rouse her from the dream, but she seemed incapable of releasing the hold the nightmare held on her.

'Sara!'

As Ashton reached for her shoulders and was about to remove the many blankets from her sleeping form, the window of her bedroom flew open, and a gust of chilling air swirled through the room, centring over her bed and immersing Ashton in cold.

A world of sound twisted and twirled against the walls of the room, shaking the tiny china figurines on the mantle and causing the clock perched there to chime as if ushering in a death toll.

The atmosphere became cloying, and Ashton felt as if he was being strangled. As bright spots danced before his eyes, his body fell to the floor and slammed against the far wall. In a daze of confusion and disbelief that this experience was anything but the wildest dream, he crawled back to the bedside and held on to the railing to stay steady.

Again the wind swirled and the furniture rattled.

'Sara, you have to wake up! Sara! Open your eyes! This isn't safe for you!'

As if a button had been flipped, the air ceased its havoc, and the world became still. Ashton didn't move from where he kneeled but stayed perfectly still, awaiting the next onslaught of supernatural activity.

Sara moaned on the bed and restlessly tossed to and fro on her pillows. Slowly, Ashton stood and reached for her shoulders once again.

'Sara, you must open your eyes. You're having a nightmare. Or maybe I'm having one, but please wake up!'

Slowly, Sara could hear running water, and she felt cold. As she awoke, she realised that her face was wet and her covers had been removed. Instantly she jerked up in the bed and looked around the room.

Ashton stood beside the bed with a wet washcloth in his hand. He looked at her with concern on his face as he slowly grinned at her. 'Welcome back to the living,' he said. 'You were having a terrible dream, and you were screaming and moaning. Are you feeling okay?'

Sara grabbed the cover around her and looked back at him with astonishment. 'Who? What? What happened?'

'I don't really know. I heard you screaming and came running in here because I thought something was wrong. I tried to wake you up, but you were really dreaming!'

'How did I get wet? And why were the covers…'

'Gone?' I took them off because you seemed to be having trouble breathing. I thought you were too hot, hence the washcloth and water. Did you know your windows can open by themselves? Wind must have been blowing really hard 'cause your window just flew open, and the air gushed in like crazy.'

Sara groaned. She couldn't quite grasp the essence of the dream but felt certain that the opening windows weren't the result of raging winds!

'It was just a bad dream, I guess,' she said, looking anywhere but at Ashton. 'I have them sometimes, even though I don't remember what they are later. Sorry I woke you.'

'Hey! No problem. I have them too. Are you better now?'

'Yeah, I'll be okay. I'll just get some water, and I will feel better, I'm sure.'

On wobbly legs, she crawled out of the bed, but before she could take a step, her knees collapsed, and she fell into Ashton's arms. He caught her and held her steady. Sara raised her face to Ashton's, looking into his eyes. He lowered his face, and she felt certain he was going to kiss her.

Just as she parted her lips, a raging wind once again swept across the room, dragging icy tendrils across her body, chilling them both.

She stepped back from Ashton and crossed her arms to warm them then stepped around him and headed for the stairs. There was no doubt in her mind that one should never fool around with Father Nature!

Chapter 7

'Bulls are out again,' said Ross when he shuffled into the store the next morning. 'Don't know what kind of fence it's gonna take to keep 'em in, but he's gotta come up with somethin' fast. Someone's gonna hit 'em on the road if he ain't careful.'

Lem slowly raised his head from the stick he was whittling. Looking around the store, he turned to answer Ross, but Marian interrupted him before he could say a word.

'What in the world are those cows doing?' Before waiting for a reply, she continued, 'I'd expect this sort of thing in the spring if there was a field of heifers next door, but by golly, the wind will chill ya to the bone, and these animals are just as feisty as ever.'

She turned and walked to the rear of the store, shaking her head and muttering to herself as she went. Lem, Ross, and Herb watched her go but never said a word or raised an eyebrow at her mumblings. They were used to her rather spastic outbursts.

'You'd think someone ran 'em out of the pasture,' Lem finally said, after thinking on the situation a bit. 'The fence ain't down, and they seem to just walk out into the road. 'Course he's got 'em separated from each other, so I guess someone would have to open two gates.'

'You say the fence ain't down?' questioned Herb as he picked up his knife and whittling stick to join Ross. 'That's kinda far-fetched, don't ya think? Opening two gates and running out two bulls? 'Specially the size of them beasts.'

'Ye-a-p,' came the reply from both men who joined him at the table.

'But then again,' Herb continued without looking up from his knife stroke, 'someone could be causing mischief or Lloyd could just be forgettin' to lock the gate. He's getting up in years, ya know. Could be that when he feeds in the mornings, he just doesn't close the gate good. They push 'em open and hightail it out to visit.'

'Could be,' said Lem. This idea was seconded by Ross, who simply shook his head.

'Course, the other thought about mischief is that some of them boys from the high school just don't have enough to do, and they are causing trouble. Zach McIntire's boys are always up to something. Don't mean no harm, I guess, but they're always doin' something to stir up trouble,' Herb said, appearing that such a long speech had left him winded. He inhaled a deep breath and settled deeper in his wooden chair.

Each of the three men had a particular chair of his own around the table. It had been that way for years, and those who entered the store to enjoy a bite of lunch or a quick snack during the evening knew that if one of them was in the store, then the chair was reserved just for him. There were other chairs near and around the table, but these three never moved. When the potbellied stove cranked up in the winter months, the chairs simply moved closer to the heat, and the table was readjusted to conform to their placement.

''Bout time for lunch, it seems,' said Ross, putting down his stick and putting his knife back in his pocket. 'Been hankering to try something new lately. Think this should be the day.'

'What'll ya have?' asked Lem as he returned his chair to all four legs. 'Wanting to try some of Marian's chicken salad sandwiches?'

'Heaven's, I hope not,' said Herb. 'That stuff will stick to your ribs, but it'll choke ya on the way down. Better try some sardines and crackers today, Ross.'

'Ump! Not today, not ever! Sardines are fish bait or cat food, but they ain't for me! Nope! I think I'll give some of that new salad a try. What's it called?'

'Salad? Why would you want salad? Nothing but grass trimmings in salad,' Lem commented.

'Not a salad but that salad stuff with meat in it that you put on a sandwich,' Ross explained. 'You know what I mean. It's got celery, onion, pickles, and ham in it.'

'Ham salad? That what you're talking about?' Herb asked with a grin. 'That ain't nothin' new. Ham salad's been around since the dark ages!'

'Well, I'm trying it today, and I hope it ain't been around since that long—this one at least. Marian, I want a ham salad sandwich,' he announced.

'You want what?' she hollered from the back of the store. 'What'd you say? You changin' food on me in midstream?'

'I want a ham salad sandwich,' Ross repeated as he turned and winked at the other two men. 'And supersize it!' Ross leaned over and patted his knee as he guffawed in loud tones about his joke. 'I heard it on the television the other night! I've been waiting to say it to her!'

Marian was watching the scene unfold from her place in the aisle of the store that led to the back cooler. Catching on to his humour, she yodeled back, 'This ain't Burger King, but if you want to have it your way, do you want it on bread or in a tomato? Do you want it with or without extra lettuce and tomato if you do want it on bread, and would you like cheese and chips with it?'

Silence reigned in the store. A pin could have dropped and been heard as the three men just looked at each other.

'Dag-nabbit! If supersizing is so hard, just give me the usual. No wonder that newsman said it was harmful to your health! Too many choices!'

'Okay, Ross!' Marian said in reply. 'One pimento cheese with mayo coming up!'

When Sara walked into the store twenty minutes later, sandwich wrappers and chips bags littered the table, the only evidence that the men's lunchtime had ended successfully. Lem had once again pulled out his whittling stick, but Ross and Herb played a hand of cards.

Marian read yesterday's old news as the paper was mailed from the Gladesville a day late rather than being delivered by a courier the day it was printed. When the bell tinkled above the door, she looked up, grinned, and went back to reading.

'Hey, guys,' Sara sang out in salutation. 'How're you guys today?'

'Well, look what the sunshine brought us, boys!' Herb said, always glad to see her whether he wanted her to know it or not.

Sara grinned at him and wrapped her arm around his shoulder. 'Who's winning?'

'Ross is cheatin', Lem ain't playin', so I'm winnin',' Herb said as everyone laughed.

'Have you noticed the weather today?' Sara absently asked as she watched Ross play the final card and win the game.

'See, I told you he was cheatin' 'cause he won,' Herb protested. 'He never wins unless he's cheatin'!'

Ross ignored Herb, and Lem knocked the wood shavings to the floor so he could sweep them up later. 'Ain't never satisfied, are you, Herb? If I play, I play too slow for you, and if Ross plays, he's cheatin' you. Maybe we just shouldn't play against you no more.'

'You couldn't do that, guys,' said Sara. 'You'd break his heart! He loves losing to you guys!'

Herb just grumbled under his breath.

'What're you doing out and about today?' Marian asked Sara, folding the paper and tossing it to the table for the men to share.

'I came to get some flour and eggs,' she replied. 'I thought I'd take some of those strawberries we froze last summer and make a pie.'

'Sounds like a great plan,' Marian remarked as she got up from her stool behind the counter. 'I've got flour that is fairly fresh and some new eggs. Jane Somers brought a bunch in this morning. Her chickens are backwards in their laying, I think. But she's got quite a few if you want me to get you some when she comes back in.'

'These will be fine,' Sara answered as the men ignored their conversation. 'I better get some milk too. What else goes in a pie?'

Marian and Sara discussed the recipes for pies and cakes as well as crusts for the pies and the advantages of using pre-made pie crusts that many stores carried in the freezer section. Marian admitted that Ms Irma, her mother, would never have allowed such a monstrosity in her store, so pre-made pie crusts, whether convenient or not, had never been added to the grocery's list of commodities.

Around the paper, the men swapped stories and newspaper pages. They pretended not to listen to the women's conversation, but because the store's size was not extremely large, they had little choice. They weren't concerned with pies or how one was made, and except for the fact that their youngest and newest arrival in the area was asking, they probably would have paid little or no attention to the women at all.

Yet there was something about the little sprite that kept all the men on their toes. They were concerned for her welfare as well as her happiness, so something as small as making a pie was their concern too.

'My wife used to add a pinch of baking soda or powder to her pie fixin',' Ross said to no one in particular. 'Boy that was good pie.'

Lem added that his daughter was a great pie baker, but living so far away, he rarely tasted pie anymore. Herb remarked that Marian couldn't make pie like Ms Irma had, but hers was still enjoyable when she bothered to make one.

It occurred to Sara, who was only half listening to Marian's instructions, that perhaps the men would enjoy it if she made them a pie. With that in mind, she quickly doubled her ingredient list and hurriedly bade them goodbye.

In the truck, she jotted down the ideas that Marian had offered, as well as the instructions for the crust in the notebook she kept on the truck seat and, looking both ways, put the truck into gear.

She pulled onto the road and started for home with more gusto than she had begun her journey. She was determined that the strawberry pie she'd imagined earlier would soon be two: one for her buddies at the store and one for Ashton and herself with their dinner that night.

Ashton was still visiting at Elizabeth's Place because Emmett had yet to discover the reason the car would not start. He'd replaced, remade, and just about completely reassembled every piece of the engine without any success. Since the mystery was a personal challenge for him, he'd promised Ashton the work was not going to be expensive, but if the car ever ran again, it would be like new.

That wonderful word *if* was the key to Ashton's departure from Crawdad and Elizabeth's Place, and since he was enjoying his stay, he admitted to Emmitt that he wasn't in a hurry about finding Red Belle's cure.

Sara whistled as she drove along, a new pastime for her. Though the tune was rarely recognisable, even to her, she enjoyed the music she could bring to her ears. She rounded a curve and swerved to avoid a pothole. That was when the bull stepped out into the road, causing her to overcompensate the wheel to miss the bovine. She lost control of the truck, careening across the road, down the ditch, and into the fence-lined pasture, wet from several days' rain.

Her head hit the steering wheel as she reached for her bag of groceries. All she could think of was her eggs and their possible damage as the truck hit first a fence post and then a rather large groundhog hole. The truck came to a stop with an abrupt lurk, causing Sara to pitch forward and slam backwards in the seat. The eggs, flour, and milk blundered to the floor, a mess of ingredients that would never find a way to a mixing bowl, and Sara's head banged into the cab's window where it stayed as blood trickled down the glass. Like the bag of groceries, Sara was shaken in a heap on the truck seat, but she didn't know the degree of her damage because she had passed out the minute the eggs hit the floor.

Chapter 8

Late afternoon sunlight streamed on her face as Sara opened her eyes. Her head felt like an elephant had used it for a cushion, and her arm and shoulder were burning as if on fire. Try as she might, Sara couldn't seem to sit up. What had happened to her? She just couldn't make her mind remember.

She listened to her surroundings to try to understand where she was. She slowly replayed the events in her mind, but with the exception of a notion to make a pie, she could remember nothing of her day.

As she tried to roll over and perhaps gain her balance to sit up, she moaned out loud. Her whole body hurt like she'd been thrown from a racing horse! She wiggled her toes inside her boots. Nothing seemed to be amiss there.

Next she tried to move her legs, and while they didn't hurt, they did seem to be tied down with something heavy around them. She knew her right shoulder and arm hurt, so she tried the left one instead.

Slowly, she raised it to her face, where she felt her face and neck.

Sara was relieved to find that the left side of her body seemed unaffected from the disagreeable havoc the right side seemed to have endured. Holding her head with her left hand, she rolled to her right hip and endeavored to sit.

Her body was racked with pain, and the noise from her throat announced it to the world, though no one seemed around to hear the pronouncement. Finally, she was leaning haphazardly to one side of her body. From the balance gained by leaning on her right hip, she bent her legs under her and gained a bit of leverage with her knees.

To Sara, hours had passed trying to get up from the ground. She still wondered how she had gotten on the ground to begin with, and she looked slowly around the area to see if one of her horses was nearby.

No horse could be seen, but a wooden wheel was propped up behind her. It seemed to be a buggy wheel and a…Could it be? A carriage?

What would she be doing in a carriage? This was really a most confusing day! Her body was aching and her head was bursting, and then she discovered a carriage! How weird!

Holding her right arm to her side, she crawled on her knees to the side of the carriage wheel and inspected the overturned vehicle. Suddenly, the idea of her truck came to mind, but it was nowhere to be found. She closed her eyes as she tried to sort the whole dilemma out, but because her head was bursting in white lights of pain, she gave up and turned herself to sit with her back against the buggy wheel.

The sun was too bright even in its watery stage, and she bowed her head and closed her eyes. Surely this must be some kind of wild dream. Again, she forced herself to revisit the steps of her day, and again, she gave up in frustration. Somewhere in her muddled mind, she knew that the truth would present itself, but for the moment, only a small nap could help her.

She sat there for quite a while, half dozing on the ground. The air seemed cooler and the daylight less bright when she demanded her eyes to open. Though she was stiff and sore, her sense of preservation pushed her to make an attempt to stand.

Agony coursed through her limbs, but even as tears trickled down her face, she forced herself to get to her knees and, with her left arm, pull herself up with the help of the wooden wheel. Slowly, leaning into the buggy and breathing rapidly in pain, she gradually made her way into a standing position.

Now what was she supposed to do, she thought. She really couldn't move away from the buggy because it was her crutch at the moment. She suddenly giggled. A buggy was her security blanket! How funny! How silly! And just as suddenly, she started to cry great sobs, even though she didn't understand exactly why she cried.

Her newfound strength of only moments ago gave way too soon, and she felt herself sliding back towards the ground. Yelling at herself inside her mind, she demanded that she stand as tall as possible and hold on to what leverage she had by clinging to the wooden floor of the carriage.

She leaned her head against the cold wood and tried to move her right arm, but it wouldn't respond to her mind's command. Darkness was slightly slipping in around her, and she knew she had to find her cell phone to call for help.

Unfortunately, her cell was nowhere to be found on the left side of her body, and reaching into the pocket of her right…Wait! Where were her jeans? What was this outfit she wore?

With eyes open wide, Sara glanced down at the shoes on her feet and the dress that met them at her ankles. She noticed for the first time that both hands were clad in supple leather gloves, and lace adorned her wrists.

What in the world had happened to her? She gasped for air as everything she thought she knew about her clothing, her surroundings, and her person suddenly took a nosedive. Where was she? Who was she?

Trying to hold some control of her overwhelmed emotions, she bit her lip in consternation. Just as reality, or what semblance of reality she held, was slipping away, she felt the ground shake under her. Wonderful! Now she was experiencing an earthquake! Maybe that was what caused this nightmare to begin with, though it didn't answer any of the questions about the weird changes around her.

'Sara,' a voice behind her called as the thundering earth quit vibrating. 'Sara, dear, are you okay?'

She tried to turn and face the voice but only succeeded in unbalancing herself and falling with a breathtaking thud to the ground. The moan she tried so hard to hold inside escaped in torturous groans.

Kind hands lifted her back and shoulders from the hard ground. She felt strength brush her cheek through the gloves that held them. Sara tried to open her eyes and look at her rescuer, but she couldn't seem to find the energy to do so. Instead, she gave herself over to the darkness that embraced her.

* * *

Samuel Cranston pulled the reins of his horse to a stop and jumped to the ground where Thomas and Houston kneeled at Sara's side. He raced to her, tromping the edges of her dress with his riding boots as he did.

Houston had already removed his shirt and wrapped it around her head to staunch the blood seeping from her brow. She was as white as the snow; no bright pinkness showed on her cheeks, and only the long black lashes of her closed eyes gave colour to her face.

He pushed the hair from her forehead as he carefully pushed the makeshift bandage aside briefly. The blood was soaking spots into the cloth, so he pulled it back in place. Looking at Houston and Thomas, he scooped the tiny woman in his arms and strode to his horse where he handed her off to Thomas before he mounted. Thomas carefully laid her in his arms as he sat stiffly in the saddle, then he and Houston also mounted.

As the three men rode hard toward Elizabeth's Place, Houston watched the way Samuel held Sara. Though they were betrothed, they had yet to set a date for their wedding, and inwardly, Houston hoped they never would. He loved Sara and had for many years.

Houston Thurman was a part of this land. He had lived on many of these lands for years as the son of the owner, and now he continued to live nearby as the friend of the new owner, William Alexander Cooper. William and his wife Elizabeth had built the new house over the hill from his parents' place only a few years ago, although his parents had passed almost a decade ago.

Houston had remained on the farm after they were gone, but growing older and lonelier, he had traveled to other regions of the States, finding himself a prolific mapmaker and, therefore, a wealthy one.

Together with his partners Thomas Sunderland and Samuel Cranston, Houston had returned to his home county. He found much of his father's and uncle's properties sold to others and immediately claimed the remaining acreage. It was a miracle of God that his old friend from school, William Cooper, had been farsighted enough to invest in the outlying property that he had often visited with his friend during school breaks and hunting retreats.

The four friends surrounded themselves with beauty; the beauty of nature was at their beck and call, and the beauty of Elizabeth and her friends who visited was the icing on the cake.

The horses fled down the hills and through the lush greenness of the valleys. Already the foliage was beginning to turn colours, and fall's breath was even now turning the air cooler. Why Sara had chosen this afternoon to visit the Marstons he didn't understand, but thankful their deer scouting had taken them in her path. Later he promised himself he would return to find what had happened to the carriage, but for now, he silently prayed his long-time friend would be okay.

Up ahead of him, Thomas urged his horse into a faster gait as he saw a gate to the right. Knowing that Samuel wouldn't dare to jump the fence with Sara in his arms, only a gate would allow them access to the bordering property.

Slipping from the saddle, he agilely grabbed the loop and swung the gate open at the same time that Houston, a superb horseman, took the fence and landed gracefully. Samuel entered the gateway, and Thomas followed, pulling the rickety closure shut.

He watched the riders in front of him as he mounted his bay mare. Most men preferred to ride stallions or geldings, but he would pen his mare against any steed in the area. He quickly caught up to the others but still lagged behind.

What had happened to Sara back there? His first question was why was she using the farm buggy instead of her own mare. She loved to ride and sat a horse quite well. Considering the wet land, why would her choice of transportation to the Marstons' be such a conveyance rather than a horse?

He admired Sara, perhaps more than was his right to do so. It was understood through the years that at the right time, Sara and Samuel would wed—a notion that he wasn't sure made either of them completely happy.

They were, in fact, complete opposites. Where Sara was spunky and full of life, Samuel was quiet and moody. Sara rode hell for leather, and Samuel carefully picked his way. When fox hunting, Sara wanted to be at the front of the pack, but Samuel preferred to ride with the hill toppers.

Even at dances, Samuel would often seek the gentlemen to chat while others captured Sara's hand. Billiards and drink were more his style where horses and dogs were hers. Sara was a quiet beauty who never put on pretense while Samuel wanted the limelight and preened more than just a bit.

Physically, the two couldn't be any more different. Samuel stood over six feet tall while tiny Sara did well to reach a solid five feet. Sara had dark eyes and hair that accented her creamy skin; Samuel's head was a mass of fiery red hair, and his skin was covered in freckles, a point that he hated.

Still Samuel was a kind and friendly fellow. Thomas couldn't fault his independence or his allegiance to his friends, community, or God. The couple just didn't fit in so many ways, but he guessed he should simply concur that opposites attract.

As the group reached the yard of the house belonging to their mutual friend William Cooper, Thomas watched as the concerned Samuel jumped from his mount with Sara and ran to the house. Thomas realised that whether the couple fit in his eyes or not, he was certain that Samuel cared for Sara and was even now proving his concern for her.

Samuel took the steps to the front door two at a time and kicked it open with his booted foot. Of all the times for Sara to get into trouble, why did it have to be today? He was supposed to meet Ralph Herd about some horses, and now this would keep him from making the scheduled appointment. He knew he could have sent Thomas or Houston to carry Sara while he rode to the Herds' place, but appearances would not have held him in high favour if he'd done that.

So now he had to decide whether to leave her in Elizabeth's capable hands and ride like the wind to Herds' place, or if he should send a groom to tell Mr Herd of this inconvenience. Why couldn't Sara just stay in the house like other girls and do some sewing instead of gallivanting around the countryside? What was he to do with her if she couldn't learn to obey his rules?

Chapter 9

As Samuel had expected, Elizabeth and her younger cousin Millie Harrison immediately took charge of Sara when Samuel appeared in the entryway of the house. Grabbing pillows and blankets, they bid Samuel to lay Sara on the sofa in the parlour and sent Sadie, the maid, to the kitchen for water and towels.

In addition, Elizabeth called Seth, the butler of sorts in the house, to fetch the doctor from town to see to Sara. It was quite easy for Samuel to look concerned because, in fact, he was concerned. He was somewhat concerned with Sara's state but overly concerned about the meeting he was about to miss should he be forced to stay and play the grieving suitor.

As he had hoped, Elizabeth saved him from his misery, asking Millie to show him out of the parlour. Samuel liked Millie. She was sweet and contained around gentlemen, always ready to lend a helping hand to others as well.

She took Samuel's arm and gently pulled him towards the door. Thinking him concerned for Sara, Millie uttered soothing nonsense words to him and told him not to fear. He looked down at the blonde woman who had a formidable stature for one so young and promised he would try to get himself together. He would do this by riding should anyone wonder where he was.

With a pat to Millie's hand and a slight smile on his face, Samuel made his exit of the house as servants quickly produced all the needed items to secure the precious Miss Sara. He closed the door with a feeling of freedom, mounted his horse, and rode like the wind for the meeting he was determined to make.

Inside the house, Elizabeth paced the floor, wondering when the doctor would arrive. Sara hadn't stirred at all since she'd been brought into the parlour. Her skin was so pale and her hands cold. Elizabeth knew that time was of the essence for the girl to mend, and frustration was mounting on her part.

She heard the opening of the door and glanced towards the entryway to see Millie return. She said something to one of the serving girls, and she left by the opposite door, gaining entrance through to the dining room.

Millie was a strange girl, Elizabeth thought. She often pretended shyness around others, though nothing could be further from the truth of her personality. William had commented more than once recently that she seemed a girl with dark thoughts and something up her sleeve. Sweet William, however, would never have voiced these assumptions aloud to anyone but her, and even then, he tried to make light of it.

William was her perfect soul mate. He was caring and sweet, a solid gentleman with ambitions of a statesman. He was…well, her William. As though her thoughts had conjured him, her handsome husband rushed into the parlour, taking her hands in his.

'How is she?' he immediately inquired after her friend. 'Has she stirred or awakened?'

'No, William, and I am so worried about her.'

Elizabeth dropped his hand, and together they walked to the sofa. Picking up the wet towel, Elizabeth patted Sara's forehead as William took her hand and rubbed it

'She's as cold as ice,' he said. 'Do you think another blanket would help chase the chill? Are you cold, darling?'

'I don't think the room is cold. I think it is just her, but I will ask that the fire be stoked. Would you stay with her while I find Millie?'

'That's silly. I will stoke the fire and stay by Sara's side at the same time. You find Millie if you need her, but I can take care of the fire. Just because we have people to wait on us doesn't mean we have to make them crazy running after things.'

Elizabeth's tinkling laugh resounded in the room.

'I know that and you know that, but do the servants know that? They are so thrilled to have jobs and a reason to work that they are disappointed when I don't ask them to do things.'

William chuckled at her remark. Neither of them was accustomed to servants, but with a large house that had the potential of housing so many, society decreed that servants be used. The post-war economy had made life difficult for so many that the turn of the century had been greeted with optimism of employment. William was just relieved that he could do his share in building the States again.

A moan from the couch brought his attention to Sara.

Elizabeth glided to her side and bent over her. 'Sara? Can you hear me, dear?' She bent near her and spoke softly to not startle her. 'Sara dear. Can you answer me?'

Again the young woman groaned and attempted to raise her hand to her forehead. Her eyes remained closed.

'Sara,' William whispered. 'Elizabeth and I want you to open your eyes now. Can you do that?'

Sara could hear the voices in the background of her throbbing head. One voice did sound somewhat familiar, but the other didn't register in her memory. But wait! Had the male voice called one of them Elizabeth?

Sara tried valiantly to open her dark brown eyes, but try as she might, her eyes remained closed as her mind reeled in swirling layers of greys and blacks. She tried to talk to the people who she sensed stood over her, but only garble seemed to come out of her mouth.

'Honey, what are you trying to tell me?' Elizabeth said, reaching for her right hand under the cover. 'Are you warm?'

'Ahh!' Sara groaned.

William instantly sought to comfort her by cradling her hand and arm gently. 'I think you've broken your arm, Sara. It is very swollen and turning blue. I think we should raise it slightly unless it hurts you too badly. Elizabeth, let's prop it on that pillow.'

The handcrafted pillow was slid in place as Sara's brow broke out in a sweat. Her cheeks became paler than imaginable, and as William and Elizabeth watched, she bit her lip.

'Oh, where is the doctor?' Elizabeth questioned as a knock came from the front door. 'Oh, there he is surely!'

The doctor was ushered into the parlour and, after much examination of Sara, announced she had indeed broken her arm in at least two places. With wooden slates and cloths, he wrapped her arm to secure it and promote the healing. He also discovered at least one broken rib and a possible concussion.

After leaving her a bottle of laudanum for pain relief, he was thanked profusely by the Coopers and escorted out the door by William.

'Tell me the truth, Doctor,' William said. 'Do you think Sara will recover? What is the prognosis?'

Dr. Whitman looked at William with a grave face.

'The young lady is strong and young, which are two things in her favour. But anytime there is a broken bone, there is a high risk of infection and blood poisoning. I'll return tomorrow to check her out. Her head is going to hurt her for quite some time due to the lick she took. That's why she won't open her eyes. The light hurts her head. Put her in a dark room and make her as comfortable as possible. She's made of sturdy stuff, I would bet. It will just take time.'

William thanked the doctor again and returned to the parlour, where he did his best to reassure Elizabeth. Sara was moved to her room upstairs, and while the fire was laid and tended in her room, the lights were not lit that night. Thanks to the medicine, she slept through the night, but Elizabeth insisted that her lady's maid stay by her side just to make sure.

Chapter 10

Much to the relief of everyone in the house, Sara's injuries weren't serious enough to hold her at bay for long. With tender ribs and a sling to protect her arm, she was up exploring within a couple of weeks' time. The days between the accident and the eventual recovery seemed like decades to her as she lay in bed, waited on hand and foot. During this time, when she was awake and able, she listened to the house staff and occasional visitors to try and piece together what had happened, where she was, and, saints preserve her, what year it was!

It became quickly obvious even to her muddled mind that she was not in the twenty-first century the moment her lady's maid, Grace, asked her to use the chamber pot! In addition, there was no light switch, no electric heat, and absolutely no cell phone!

But how did this happen? Was there a possibility of a parallel universe, or had she just hit her head so hard that she had shaken her brain to the point of dysfunctional realism? While this baffling and rather overwhelming ridiculous mess seemed to be 'real' to those surrounding her, Sara was acceptant of the conditions. In her opinion, another nod towards her possible insanity!

She gradually picked up the names that went with the faces as they came to visit her. Much of the time she would pretend to be asleep so that she could watch them as they sat beside the bed. It was amazing the things one could learn by being silent!

For instance, Elizabeth Cooper was as lovely as she had imagined. She was beautiful on the outside, but her heart was captivating. She thought of others' welfare first and never ceased to pray at Sara's bedside for her recovery.

William, oh William! William was a handsome man in this mixed-up time as he was in her time. It was very obvious that he adored his wife, he tolerated one cousin named Millie, and he was as tender-hearted as she had come to love in her world.

Millie was exasperating with her pretense of concern and even a bit evil as she seemed occupied in doing what could cause more pain to Sara if she thought that Sara slept. Therefore, Sara learned little about the tall blonde because when she approached the bed, Sara made certain her eyes were open!

Grace was very kind. A beauty of a child-woman, Grace was gentle and had a sweet disposition. She would read to Sara to pass the hours but always cautioned her if a funny part of the story was coming so that Sara could hold the pillow to her hurt ribs. Though she was supposed to be a paid servant, Grace was rapidly becoming a friend and confidant. She secretly helped Sara rise from the bed and begin to walk, even though William had warned her against such shenanigans.

Then there were William's friends who visited her every day. Apparently, at the turn of the twentieth century—according to Grace, who thought her head injury must have taken part of her memory—Samuel was Sara's boyfriend. However, Sara found that he wasn't her favourite of the men because he seemed self-centred and preoccupied at each visit. How anyone but the vain Millie could enjoy his company was beyond Sara!

He was tall and red-headed and apparently could have a temper to match his hair. He often appeared to have been indulging in drink before his visit and awkwardly stood several feet from her bed rather than sitting close by in the chair. No, Samuel wasn't her choice of beaus, regardless of what year the calendar showed.

He was often accompanied with Thomas and Houston. If the three were together, the visits were very short and businesslike, but if Thomas or Houston dropped in to see her alone, the time was merrily spent with some fascinating tale of hunting, riding, or dancing, which they both promised to entertain her with upon her recovery.

Sara instantly liked Houston. He was tall and well-built with a rugged stride and confident air. He wasn't vain or boastful as Samuel could be, but he was kind and tender-hearted like William. There were many similarities to William, but he was also a great deal like someone else she knew. She just couldn't put a name to the face she compared him to in her dreams.

Houston always brought her wild flowers to brighten her room. Often, if Grace was listening to their conversation, she would hear the chuckles from the young girl. Houston definitely had a gift with humour.

And finally there was Thomas. Thomas seemed a bit shy at first, but soon warmed to Sara as he realised that she wasn't likely to succumb while he visited. He, like Houston, was much warmer to her than Samuel, and Thomas appeared to have a true interest in her welfare.

Grace often spoke of Thomas with a broad smile on her face, and it was obvious even in Sara's delusional state of mind that Grace dreamed of waltzing through the ballroom in his arms. Too bad that station in life kept them apart, for Thomas seemed equally as interested in her. Maybe if Sara's state of time change continued, she could find a way to bring them together!

Oh! What balderdash! Was she really a victim of time travel? Could she really be just plain nutty? If only she could wake up from this incredibly disturbing dream or sleep and awake back in her world, surrounded by the simple things she understood!

Grace appeared at her bedside and spoke quietly so as not to startle her. 'Miss Sara? Are you ready to eat something? I have some broth for you and some tea.'

Distraught by her musings, Sara pretended to be asleep, but Grace was quick as a wink and roused her once again.

'I know you are playing possum, ma'am! I also heard Mrs Elizabeth tell Mr William that she was planning on seeing you after she had luncheon. I think you should try to eat something so you have some strength, don't you?'

Sara moaned and opened her eyes to see Grace's bright smile beaming at her. She knew that her deception might work with others, but no longer would it work with Grace. Accepting the girl's help, Sara scooted up in the bed and leaned against it. She really was tired of broth but obligingly accepted the cup and swallowed the soup. The tea was always the best part of the liquid meal because it was strong and sweet, something she really needed to clear her head.

Before she was finished, Elizabeth glided into the room, smelling of lavender and looking like a queen. 'Well, don't you look grand today, Sara?' she tweeted as she unceremoniously seated herself in the chair. 'I'm so glad to see the colour in your cheeks again. How's the arm today?'

Sara wanted to tell her the colour in her face was probably as much from the sugar and heat of the tea as good health but didn't disappoint her. Instead she grinned at her new-found friend and leaned back against the headboard of the bed.

'I think I feel some better today. I'm not usually such a baby about being sick or hurt, and I think I am becoming quite spoiled. I should get up and help you do things in the house instead of making folks tend to me!'

'Don't be silly.' Elizabeth chuckled. 'Besides, everyone deserves to be pampered once in a while. Just relax and get back on your feet slowly. Perhaps you would like to sit in the upper sitting room tomorrow in the sun if it blesses us with its presence. The days are already getting greyer with cold.

'I do look forward to the coming season though. Christmas will be here before we know it. Won't it be fun to see the house in festive wear again? And the bonfire isn't long away, you know. You'll have that to look forward to in the next few weeks. Do you have any idea what you'll wear to the ball that follows it?

'Do hurry up and get better, Sara! I miss your company in the evenings. Don't tell anyone, but I am so tired of playing hostess to Millie and her friend Caroline, but last night they told me they would be here until after the ball.'

Caroline was a friend of Millie's from Savannah who had arrived two nights past. She had a laugh like a shrill bird that could be heard from the drawing room. Sara had not yet met her, but from Elizabeth's description, the woman was obviously an empty-headed twit. She spoke only of her clothing and only wanted to dance and preen for the 'rich and elite gentlemen' who would surely be found at Elizabeth's ball.

Elizabeth told Sara several funny stories but excused herself quickly when she discovered her visit was tiring Sara. When she left the room, Sara was instantly alone as she enjoyed the time she spent with this woman.

It occurred to her that instead of merely listening to Elizabeth, she should be asking questions that could produce answers to the mystery of her death on that fateful night so many years before...Well, that couldn't be though, could it? That day hadn't yet happened for Elizabeth was still alive—so to speak!

Suddenly, the idea of twisting time came to Sara. Since she knew some sketchy outlines of the evening that Elizabeth died, perhaps, just maybe, Sara could intervene and change the circumstances of the day.

But what did she really know about the incident? She pondered. She knew only what William had related to her: there was a party, there was a ride in the moonlight, and there was an accident, a horrible, terrible accident that left Elizabeth a sweet memory. If only Sara could determine when the party was, who would be there, and what the planning of the demise was, then she could interrupt it just long enough to prevent Elizabeth from leaving the house. William would be spared the heartache of the day, and then, at his death, whenever that happened, his spirit would be free to join the saints in heaven.

Oh! How Sara's heart filled with joy! Of all the gifts she could give to William for all his kindness and love, this was one that could actually become a reality. She knew the possible side effects of tampering with history, but she was willing to forego caution and restore his heart.

She giggled with anticipation, so much so that Grace asked her if she was feeling well. Oh! Was she ever! Giddy with the thrill of adventure, Sara obediently took her medicine and plotted and planned on ways to get better sooner than expected and make this project a successful one!

Chapter 11

As the days that followed turned into weeks, Sara's health grew rapidly better, so much so that outings outside were a daily habit with Houston at her side or Grace leading the way. In between a visitor to claim her time, Elizabeth regaled her with her stories of holidays past or ideas of the decorating of Elizabeth's Place.

But before the holiday season truly kicked off, William announced a party to be held for neighbours, special friends, and family members. Sara was excited about the prospects of the party, but Samuel quickly staunched any ideas of gaiety on her part.

'How can you dance with only one arm, Sara?' he asked on more than one occasion when the event was still in the planning stages. 'You are all but an invalid, so I wouldn't get my hopes up to enjoy the evening.'

'She's not a cripple, Samuel,' Houston remarked. 'She simply has a broken arm that is on the mend quite well, according to the doctor's last remarks. I think even in a sling, she could still enjoy the festivities of the gala.'

'Gentlemen, gentlemen, a lady can always find a way to enjoy a dance.' Elizabeth interrupted their sparring. 'Sara is definitely not an invalid, Samuel, and she certainly enjoys a soirée!'

'That is her problem most of the time,' responded Samuel in a huff. 'She needs to learn her limitations in dancing as well as mischief. How she will ever fit into my lifestyle is beyond me.'

'She isn't a horse to be put in your herd,' said Thomas with a startled laugh. 'She is an active lady with a great imagination and a head for the exploits. That is part of what makes Sara who she is.'

'You sound as if you have a penchant for her escapades.' Elizabeth chuckled.

'I do admire Sara's wit,' Thomas began, but was interrupted by Houston. 'And her beauty and charm as well.'

'Okay, so she is quite the woman!' Elizabeth couldn't help egging on the friends, though Samuel seemed more than a bit miffed at the turn of conversation.

'I just don't think a respectful woman should be so full of life! She should be quiet and reserved,' he commented.

'Oh, you are so right,' said Elizabeth. 'It is better for one to blend in with the wall than to have a unique personality. Why, it might outshine her husband!'

Houston, Thomas, and Elizabeth enjoyed a hearty laugh as Samuel stormed out of the room just as William arrived.

'What's stuck in Samuel's craw?' he asked as he hugged his wife and smiled down at her.

She gazed up at him lovingly but still with a smirk on her face. 'We have insulted his majesty's perception of what a perfect woman is, I do believe,' she said. 'Samuel wants Sara to be demure and lifeless while everyone else has a good time at the party. Honestly, sometimes one would think he's not known her almost all her life. He should be adjusted to her whims and ways.'

'Perhaps Samuel needs to change his horse if he finds his with too much spirit!' Houston said. 'I enjoy a woman who can think for herself and enjoy a good laugh, but Samuel obviously doesn't know how wonderful those attributes are.'

William cleared his throat and hastened to change the subject as he saw Sara coming down the stairs. She was a beauty, he had to admit, and she was a blessing to Elizabeth, which made her even more of a gem in his eyes.

'Sara, my dear, how are you feeling?' he asked.

'Better than ever!' she replied as she looked around the room and smiled at those present. 'What are all of you up to this fine afternoon?'

'As little as possible,' Thomas answered, 'which makes all of us slackers who need to return to work. Ladies, please forgive us, but we must get back to business!'

At their exit from the room, Sara chose a chair near the bright window and picked Elizabeth's thoughts for Christmas gifts for the men.

'Have you heard Thomas or Houston mention anything at all they'd like to see under the tree this year?' she queried as Elizabeth's needle flew in and out of the piece she worked. Behind her, a lovely decorative tapestry hung in vivid colours of girls enjoying the autumn leaves and a picnic on the ground. The afternoon sun graced their heads, and their laughter was almost audible. Elizabeth had crafted the picture almost a year ago.

'No one has said a word this year, including you, Sara, so frankly, I am at a loss as to what would be gifts. No doubt, baked goods will be ideal for the neighbours, and hopefully, chocolates for William will set right. That way I can help myself to his package!'

Gales of laughter rose from the room at Elizabeth's idea for someone else's gift that she could nab. It was then that Millie joined their group, and though the young woman's prime demeanor and personality overshadowed the gaiety, she did join in with their ideas for surprises.

Teatime arrived, a tradition that Elizabeth continued as a remembrance of her mother and grandmother. Tiny finger sandwiches of frothed cream and autumn berries joined tarts and cookies for a delicious repast. The tea was steeped just right by Cook, and the girls thoroughly enjoyed their time together.

Sara stifled a yawn behind her hand. 'My apologies,' she said. 'I think I've become quite lazy since my accident. Every afternoon I grow so sleepy after tea that I can barely hold my eyes open.'

'Perhaps you'd enjoy a walk around the garden,' announced Elizabeth, but Sara denied the adventure, saying she was too tired to walk.

'I'll join you, cousin,' said Millie, who gathered a shawl to drape around her shoulders.

Having little excuse to not take the offered walk, Elizabeth put her needlework aside and hugged Sara's shoulders. 'Enjoy your nap,' she said as she joined hands with Millie and headed for the front door. 'I'll see you at dinner.'

Sara remained in the ladies' parlour and basked in the afternoon sun. She knew she should enjoy it while she could for the fall weather promised grey skies and colder temperatures on the horizon. As she sat and relaxed, the door to the side of the house opened and closed, and multiple footsteps tromped in the wooden hallway.

Voices could be heard, and though she had early on been taught not to eavesdrop on conversations, she really didn't have the energy to move from her position. So she listened to the conversation that ensued.

'I don't think this plan will work. I don't care how badly you want that land,' a male voice said. It was a man's voice Sara didn't recognise, but the one who answered was well-known to her.

'Regardless of what it takes, I must have that land. Land marks your wealth, and I have never had intentions of being poor! Wherever that letter is, find it. It is in this house, somewhere, for Elizabeth mentioned it to William the other night as we all left from the dinner table. She said the deed was with the letter she had, and the name on the deed was missing.

'I need that letter and that deed. That land is mine, should be mine, and I won't sleep until I have it in my possession. I am positive that valuables are on that land, besides the rich dirt for crops. Find it! And kill anyone who tries to stop you from obtaining it!'

There was a grunted reply, but Sara couldn't hear the response as boots clicked away down the hallway. Sara couldn't believe her ears! The vicious greed that she had just overheard left her breathless. To hear plots for stealing property was one horrible thing, but to know that it could encompass murder was another thing entirely!

She felt light-headed and shocked. To think, right here in her home, this evil could be afoot. And to think that those conspiring to commit it were people she not only knew but had held a deep regard of affection and respect for during her life! How could anyone be so vile? How could she have been so dense? To think that she had almost been bound to this man for life was more than she could comprehend for the voice that she'd heard had belonged to none other than Samuel!

* * *

Millie and Elizabeth walked into the cool wind that unexpectedly seemed to have grown colder as the afternoon had passed. Millie still had her arm linked in the crook of Elizabeth's elbow. She chit-chatted about nothing and everything; Elizabeth wasn't listening to the nonsense but thinking instead of how she wished her companion was Sara or William or even Houston. For that matter, she'd rather be at the dogs' kennel or in the stable, a place she found great comfort in.

'Oh, it does seem so terribly cold, cousin,' Millie tweeted. 'We should walk faster to warm up ourselves.'

'If we were smart, the only place we would be walking is inside the house! It is an idea that I suggest strongly. I am turning around, in fact, and headed that way before you catch your death in that skimpy coat.'

'Oh, don't be silly.' Millie tried to smile. 'I really need to walk about, and I really shouldn't go alone. You must go with me.'

'Only towards the barn then,' Elizabeth replied. 'That way, I can check on the dogs and the horses at one time. And, too, the barn will allow us to warm up a bit before starting back to the house.'

'But the barn is so smelly, especially when it's been closed for hours. Besides, don't you and William employ people to do these labours? It is all so tiresome.' Millie pouted. 'I know! We could go to the caves. They are warm and always so pleasant to pretend inside when the wind is blowing.' Millie jerked at Elizabeth's arm, trying to lead her away from the safety of the barn and head into the woods and, eventually, the caves.

'I am not headed into any cave today! They are gloomy enough in the sunlight, much less so on a rainy day! Now, I am going to the stables or the house. You can choose which, and I will follow.' Elizabeth stood stock-still, willing Millie to make up her mind.

Millie instead stomped her foot and, with her breath foggying up the cold air, declared herself cold and turned for the house, leaving Elizabeth watching her leave.

'Well, I never!' Elizabeth said to herself, turned towards the barn, and finished her afternoon outing playing with newborn kittens and feeding kibble to the dogs.

Millie, on the other hand, was furious at the turn of events, which fueled her speed in returning to the house. She stomped into the library just in time to see Sara skipping up the stairs with more than a bit of spring in her step.

'Nothing is going right today!' Millie fretted aloud. 'That just proves that if you want something done, you have to do it yourself. And there is no time like the present!'

'Pray tell, who you're talking to, Millie?'

'Oh, Caroline, I didn't know anyone was downstairs. Have you had an enjoyable day?'

Caroline twisted a golden curl and stuck out her bottom lip. 'I must admit that the trip hasn't been a complete bust, but it hasn't been exceptionally good either,' the girl said. 'I really like Mr Houston and even Mr Samuel. I don't care overly for Mr Thomas. He seems to be quite bland. And I really find Mrs Cooper and her friend ghastly!'

'Really? Do tell! I am very interested in knowing all about how you feel. But we mustn't do it here. Let's go to my room and have tea. Then we can discuss all your thoughts.'

The sly Millie's smile spoke volumes as she sashayed from the room with Caroline in her wake. Together the girls giggled as they climbed the stairs, forgetting completely that the very lady they spoke of was the hostess of their visit.

* * *

'William, I think the idea you have is perfect for the future,' a tall grey-haired man with a deep voice said as Sara approached the library door. The room was a favourite of Sara's, at least in her present-day home. She knew that behind the door were walls of cherry bookshelves that held numerous books. Because the room was housed in the turret of the house, the second floor was likewise lined with shelving in rich wood that contained priceless porcelain antiques and rare books.

Sara paused in the hallway, wrestling with the need to alert William to what she had overheard earlier. But the man in the room held his full attention, and from the cigar smoke that was evident, there was more than one visitor with him.

Finally her instincts for good conduct won out, and she mentally promised to immediately address the matter with Elizabeth if she could be located inside the house. Otherwise, she would wait for these folks to leave, and then…

Footsteps trod on the wooden floor, and movement behind the library door alerted Sara to the withdrawal of the men. Their voices were jovial and loud, full of good humour. William led them from the room and into the main parlour of the house while Sara hid behind a curtain so she wouldn't be found. Regretfully, William was completely occupied with the visit of these men, so she silently slipped up the stairs and to the master chambers, where she hoped to find Elizabeth.

Instead she found Millie and Caroline giggling like schoolgirls in the upstairs sitting room. She briefly spoke to them before heading to her room for the brief respite. As she walked down the hallway, Millie said, 'By the by, sweet Elizabeth is probably frozen in the barn, but that was where she insisted we walk. I came back to get warm, so perhaps you should check on her!'

Turning, Sara answered that she would do just that and fetched her coat. However, as she glanced out the window, Sara was alarmed to see Elizabeth and Samuel apparently having a heated discussion in the yard. Though she couldn't hear either of their words, their body language showed the distress or disagreement they were having.

Finally, Elizabeth's arm rose to slap Samuel's face, which, upon contact, jerked to one side. As he raised his hand to stroke his cheek, Elizabeth hurriedly made an escape towards the house. Not to be outdone, Samuel reached for her shoulder to stop her departure, but in her haste, he only came away with her coat in his hand. Her arms slid from the wrap as he held the material, and she hastened into the warmth of the home's kitchen, safe for the moment.

'What in the world?' Sara questioned to the empty room. She dropped her coat and ran back down the hall to find Elizabeth was already climbing the stairs for her room. Her cheeks were flushed with more than cold as she slowed and gave Sara a weak grin.

'Are you well?' Sara asked.

Elizabeth gave her a brisk nod, a weak smile, and a 'Later' as she slid past her and entered her room, where she quickly closed the door.

Sara was left standing in the hallway with her mouth open and her mind full of questions and ideas. But more than anything, she had a sense of urgency to talk to William about what she'd seen and now what she'd witnessed. Blessed be! What else could be afoot?

Chapter 12

'I'm going riding tomorrow, ladies,' said Houston that night at dinner. He was not necessarily issuing an invitation to have them join him, but trying to lighten the tension at the meal.

'Where are you going?' Millie asked while Caroline tested each potato before selecting one for her plate from the master bowl and passing it forward. 'If the weather remains as cold, I wouldn't think the ride would be of much enjoyment.'

'You are right, Miss Millie, I am sure for a lady of delicate demeanor, that is very true. And the winds are very brisk tonight, to say the least,' Thomas countered.

'I would love to ride tomorrow if I was able,' said Sara with longing. 'I feel as if I've been trapped for years inside...'

'Don't be dramatic,' Caroline snapped. 'It's only been a day or so since your accident.'

'...Though it's only been a week or two,' Sara concluded.

'Well, why don't you try to see how you feel in the saddle,' Houston offered and then proceeded to tell those at the table where and when he would make his journey. It seemed that the small town not far from the house had a special baker that he wished to visit.

'We'll go there and back if you'd like to join me. In fact, the tavern there has a nice teatime menu if you'd like to take the time.'

Sara agreed to meet him at the stables in the morning and declared that the effort would be made, but she wouldn't go as far as to promise she could join the outing.

Samuel listened without concern; cutting his roast beef seemed more important. Millie, sitting next to him, continuously tried to get his attention, touching his sleeve or asking him if he desired another roll.

He looked up at her and smiled—the first real acknowledgement he made of any of the people partaking of the meal with him. Elizabeth saw the brief smile they gave each other. It was a smile of something more than dinner companions, and it was noticed by more than one diner.

Thomas took note of it immediately, stopping his speech about weather and animal conditions. He was so aware of it. He quickly resumed, but not before William's eyes followed his to the source of interest. Samuel and Millie noticed only each other.

Sara paid no attention but buttered her freshly baked bread and nodded at something that Elizabeth said. When the meal was over and the ladies left the gentlemen to their conversation and cigars, William wasted no time in calling Samuel on the carpet for his actions at the table.

'William, I wasn't aware that my table manners were under scrutiny. If I offended you, I apologise. However, I don't believe I did anyone any injustice, especially Miss Millie.'

'I just thought that since you and Sara were promised to each other that you would have more consideration for her feelings. You rarely pay her attention that is due your position.'

With whispered venom, Samuel hissed at William, 'I don't know that I am promised to anyone. And the last person I would consider myself tied to is Sara. She is an exasperating young woman who has too much independence for my lifestyle or needs. We've known each other for more decades than I care to remember, and each one of those decades has memories of destruction and devastation that is somehow linked to her!'

Samuel strode away from the table and out the door, leaving William and the others staring at the spot where he'd stood. Seconds later, the front door banged with a vengeance, and the men exchanged glances of query with William.

'He treats women abysmally! He cannot possibly call himself a gentleman to behave the way he does,' William said. 'He needs to make his intentions clear before he plays with the emotions of visitors and residents of Elizabeth's Place.'

'You've known Samuel for years, William. You know how he acts when he's socialising. He is brash and confident to the point of rudeness, but rarely does he behave ungentlemanly.' Thomas defended their subject.

'I agree with you, Thomas, but at the same time, I completely concur with William. Samuel hasn't been himself lately, and perhaps he has a bachelor-itis! You know how we've all egged him about getting married to Sara.'

'He has no desire to marry her! He just admitted that to me, but he hasn't, to my knowledge, mentioned it to her,' William angrily said. 'Honestly, a gentleman owes a lady that much conversation!'

'Be calm, William,' Houston said. 'While I think he owes Sara an explanation, I don't think she will be overly concerned at this development. She is a spunky girl with a head on her shoulders and a determination about her. William, I promise you, she will take this well.'

'He still owes her an explanation. That's all I will say about.'

Thomas and Houston shared a look that spoke volumes. William was as close as an older brother to Sara, and he was protective of her. Though his three friends knew this, each held a special place in his heart for the lady.

'Just don't be so hard on him. He fell quite quickly for her when they met years ago because she rode better than he did. She jumped a horse better than he could, and she was always fun. Sara doesn't primp and flirt that way other girls do. With Sara, you have a real person, but with looks, like a pretty lady.'

'Well said, Houston.' William laughed. 'But inside the pretty woman is the heart of a kitten. Don't let me find a man who will tread on that heart!'

'Hey, remember the time she put pepper in his tea? His eyes popped out for ages before he got over that,' Thomas remembered with a laugh. 'Don't know why he got so upset about it after he'd done it to Scottsford when we were in Boston!'

'Speaking of Scottsford, he and two of his buddies visited me just the other day,' William stated and went on to tell the friends of the conversation in the library. He spoke highly of the men he'd met and their ideas. Then he relayed his concerns with several of those proposed policies until Cook scooted them from the kitchen, and they were forced to take refuge in the sitting room to hear Caroline play the harp. William was encouraged to play the violin, a beautiful talent that brought tears to Elizabeth's and Sara's eyes.

As he played, Sara closed her eyes and remembered an evening not so long ago when she had been William's sole audience. He had played with an intensity that shattered her heart because he was so moved by the music. The lushness of the room was no different now than what she remembered from the room at home—brocades and thick rugs with beautiful cherry woodwork and scrumptious curtains. But the music here was truly the art. How wonderful it was to hear him play again with such life and enthusiasm and to know that the woman he played for was alive to share each melodic lyric with him.

They were perfect for each other, Elizabeth and William. Theirs was a real love that transcended the ages. Sara basked in the moment of perfect peace, but deeper still wondered when it all would come to an end.

* * *

Snow was falling beneath the grey skies the following morning so heavy that Sara didn't want to stir from her goose-down bed when Grace brought her tea and biscuits. She snuggled her pillow like a tiny child before the aroma of buttery goodness coaxed her from the covers.

'I don't think riding is a good idea this day,' Grace said with a mischievous grin. 'I think Mr Houston's bakery needs will have to be answered by Cook instead of the village baker.'

'I guess, but…Oh! I know what we can do!' Sara squealed. 'We can take the sleigh and go on a snowy sleigh ride! Get on your warmest boots and lay out a warm coat! I'll go find Houston and tell him!'

Scooting to the edge of the bed with caution for her still healing ribs and arm, Sara was ready to bounce to the floor and fly from the room in her gown. Thankfully, for her grown-up dignity, Grace stopped her before her feet hit the floor with a reprimanding glance.

'Back to bed with you!' she said. 'You know that you can't just go running about the house undressed!

Not even a tiny tot would do so! Now, eat your breakfast, and I'll go in search of Mr Houston, then I'll be back to make sure you're properly dressed for the outing. Eat!'

Wanting to pout for being treated like a child but too eager for the adventure ahead, Sara stepped back into the hand-carved rice bed while Grace placed her tray on her lap. Grace spread strawberry jam on the biscuits and added a touch of cream to the china cup of tea.

'I'll be back in just minutes. Stay in that bed until I return because Cook is complaining about the amount of china being broken by wayward diners. I think that means you! You've not broken a single plate, but the cups are a different matter.'

With a smile, Grace left Sara to eat. As she did, she traced the lip of the cup with a finger, thinking of the small amount of cups versus the number of saucers, bowls, and plates in the cabinet at home. Could she, at this time, have broken the cups that were now missing from that set? In this strange, mixed-up world that she was in, anything seemed possible.

Mere minutes later, Sara was tucked under blankets and her hands were engulfed in a warm beaver muff when she, Houston, and Grace for a chaperone headed into town. Under a sunny sky with good conditions, the journey would have taken nearly an hour, but under the conditions of the morning, the drive would be lengthy and cold. All for baked goods!

Laughing and singing merry Christmas songs, Sara urged Houston and Grace to join her. She begged for Houston to stop the sleigh for a snowball fight, but he wouldn't allow her to get any colder than her blue lips said she already was.

The three enjoyed lunch, shopped, and then, before the afternoon began to fade, began the trip home. As they got closer to Elizabeth's Place, each picked a tree to dress the house for Christmas. Sara chose a huge, tall pine while Grace selected a small cedar for the upstairs rooms. Houston promised to have someone bring a wagon and cut and carry the trees to the house while he selected one for his own home.

Sara urged him to tell her of his house, which he did with eagerness, describing the white clapboard, two-story dwelling with warmth. He told of the stone fireplace that adorned most of the centre room, connecting to the kitchen alcove and helping heat the upstairs bedrooms. He spoke with such love of the house that Sara could almost see his mother baking bread at the cast-iron stove or cutting out cookies on the wooden table that his father had cut and hewn for a wedding gift.

He spoke of the spinet and the piano that flanked the music room windows and the drawing room chairs that always creaked when one sat in them. He laughed about the notches in the staircase spindles where his brother had tried to chop down a pretend cherry tree so that he could grow up like George Washington; the nursery room walls were coloured with chalks and paints that left testimony of his sister Isabel's story illustrations.

Houston regaled his passengers with stories of jumping from windows on the second floor to riding horses in the creek to see which swam the best before the gates of Elizabeth's Place came into view.

Stiffly, Sara was helped from the sleigh and ushered inside the house. Grace took her coat and encouraged her to the fireplace to warm. Houston joined her, and in gales of laughter, she surprised him with a snowball she had hidden in the palm of her hands. His shriek of incredulity brought Elizabeth and William running into the room. They too were soon laughing heartedly from the outrageousness of Sara's antics.

Cook sent in hot chocolate and sliced Houston's confectionary finds for a tea of sorts, and soon the room was filled with good-natured joking and joyous fun. Declaring herself happier than a coonhound with a bone, Elizabeth told them all of the party details that would be held in two weeks.

'Two different bands will come and play, and Cook is making the most wonderful fruit cake and turkey roasts. We've had responses from most of those invited, but we still are under the fifty-guest mark. William has invited some of his colleagues and a few special guests that I haven't yet met. It should be such a fun evening! And the house will be beautiful with all the greenery hung! I'm just so excited about it!'

William reached over and squeezed Elizabeth's hand as she chirped on and on about her party. The days couldn't pass quickly enough for her as friends from far and wide would be attending the weekend of festivities.

The only folks who didn't join completely into the planning and gaiety were Caroline, Millie, and Samuel. The three of them sat on the sofa and chatted together, with Thomas going between the two groups of conversation. By the afternoon's end, those present at Elizabeth's Place were well warmed, fed, and entertained, having played games of all sorts before the dinner hour.

With Cook providing rich soups and breads, the group was completely stuffed when they retired to bed. Climbing the steps, Sara's mind reviewed her lovely day and wished that she could share that happiness with Houston, who had left for his own home with Thomas in his stead. Samuel, whom she had all but forgotten about during the day, had declined his invitation to stay at the house, but had, like the others, retreated to his own home.

She hugged herself as she climbed into bed with Grace's help. The world seemed as right as rain…but she knew the rain would surely fall, and she had only days to find a way to be the umbrella for them all.

Chapter 13

In the days that followed, the house was primed and readied with the dressings of Christmas. Massive wagons of evergreens arrived at the front door where artisans prepared bountiful wreathes, twined pine boughs around the front porch columns, and laid the swags under the windows of the second floor. Candles were nestled in the greenery and laid along mantels and window sashes. The whole house smelled of the outdoors.

Even the doors of the barn held a welcome to the season. In addition, pine cones decorated the walkways, and heavy ribbons gave a bright burst of colour to the landscape of green. Silver bells and the bells from the sleigh harnesses chimed each time the doors opened around the farm and house. A bright merriness encompassed both human and animals.

By evening, the house's occupants declared the home warm and lovely. The only thing that remained to be decorated was a tree that, according to Houston, would be delivered the following day.

Cook passed around hot cocoa and cookies as the decorating wound down, and all prepared for dinner that smelled superb.

'Make sure your hands and faces are scrubbed because there is soup and cheese biscuits to be served as well as pumpkin butter and sweet scones with berries,' the short and dumpy woman with a headful of waving grey hair proclaimed. 'I'm saving the real food for the guests!' And off she trotted back to the kitchen.

'Well, you heard the woman,' said William as he too prepared to leave the room. 'I think the tasty soup will be very filling, and then sleep will be a breeze after all we've accomplished today.'

Elizabeth grinned from ear to ear with pleasure. How silly that she should be almost giddy with anticipation of the coming weekend. Oh! How she enjoyed the holidays!

Caroline didn't seem nearly as pleased with the upcoming events when Elizabeth joined them all in the dining room. Instead, Caroline complained about her soup and seemed to detest the warm cornbread that Cook had ladled with butter. She was especially gruff in response to a question about her dress for the occasion.

'Why do I care what I wear? There won't be anyone here but some hillbillies! I should have spent the season in Charleston or Savannah, not here!'

Though her outburst made everyone around the table uncomfortable, no one responded, and the meal continued in near silence. Only Houston contributed to the conversation, and he merely questioned the opportunity for more snow.

Finally everyone filed out of the dining room with Caroline and Millie announcing their plans to retire for the evening. Elizabeth asked if anyone wished to walk for a bit before turning in, but in the end, only William strolled around the yard with her.

Houston and Thomas made a hasty exit for their respective homes, which left only Sara in the parlour. Samuel hadn't been present for dinner and wasn't seen afterwards either. Sara had to wonder about his consumption of business, especially with the party just around the corner. He seemed so preoccupied these days that there seemed little time for them to spend any time together.

Not that she honestly minded. Samuel wasn't her favourite of the gentlemen. She preferred Houston's gift for humour and his kind ways. He never seemed to tire of simply being in her presence regardless of what was transpiring. Somewhere in the back of her mind, Houston reminded her of someone else, but she couldn't quite put her finger on it just yet.

Sara turned the page on the book she was attempting to read, knowing full well she would only have to reread it the next time she found the time to read. She sat wondering about myriad thoughts, never really letting her mind settle on one before moving to another.

She heard the front door open and knew it must be Elizabeth and William returning. They obviously proceeded to their room because neither of them stopped by the parlour to say good night.

To be in love! What a thrill it must be! Sara never imagined Samuel and herself in that situation, so she longed for the day that she too could float on the breezes of happiness at the thought of a beau's name.

Gathering her book, she began up the stairs, but felt someone's presence in the hallway. She turned, feeling she was being watched, but could find nothing out of place and no one in the entryway. Still she couldn't shake the feeling that something just wasn't right.

As she gained the top step, she once again looked back to the bottom floor. Muddy footprints were visible on the floor, but the marks belonged to someone other than Elizabeth and William. For one thing, there was only one set of prints, and surely there would have been two if they belonged to the home's owners.

Deciding she had an overactive imagination, Sara hurried down the hall to her room and there found her sweet maid waiting to help her into her bedclothes. That done, she climbed into the bed, ready to sleep.

But sleep was elusive. Her mind kept repeating the many things that she had learned over the last few days, coming to dwell on the scene that Samuel had presented earlier. How could he truly feel that unkindly about people who were his friends?

When sleep did finally come to her, Sara had dreams of both the century she was presently in and the one in which she had always lived. She ran and played with her dogs through the snow, but she was dressed as she had this day. Oh, how confusing it all was. And the days were quickly ticking away until what she knew would be Elizabeth's demise. Unless fate and Sara, by some miracle, could stop time's clock and make it stand still. If not, did she dare to twist time and keep Elizabeth safe in William's arms? And would Samuel instigate another round of evil to further complicate the whole scenario?

As she tossed and turned in her comfortable bed, one thing seemed to resound over and over in her mind: Elizabeth had to be protected, and Samuel had to be stopped regardless of whether she ever found her way home again or not.

* * *

Far from feeling rested the next morning, Sara chose to spend her early morning hours in the stables. The smell of hay and the warmth of the animals made her happy and secure. She fed the horses and put apples aside for them as a treat for later. She sat on the hay bale in the centre of the hallway and leaned back against the barn wall. As tired as she was, this was a wonderful and restful place.

She could hear the dogs in the kennel barking and knew that someone was feeding them. Though the frost was thick this morning, there was no new snow, a rather disappointing thing to Sara and the dogs that looked forward to a walk out on cold mornings. The crisp air made the fox scents even more profound for the eager hounds, and on a morning such as this, the horses, the riders, the hounds, and even the foxes were feeling a lift to their spirits when excitement was just moments away.

Sara wanted to pout because she knew she wouldn't be allowed to ride on this Christmas hunt. She wouldn't even get to ride gently with the hill toppers like Samuel always wanted to do. To save her life, she couldn't understand why he insisted in riding with those of lesser ability in the saddle or experience for the hunt. She thrived in being at the front of the hunt, watching the hounds work and feeling the excitement of every jump along the way.

But this year, she was on hostess duty. That meant she would be the one left behind to manage the drinks and breakfast and to entertain the ladies and gentlemen who didn't or couldn't ride out with the hunt. Instead of her lovely riding suit, she would be stuffed into a corset and frock that was appropriate for a lady to wear. Elizabeth would join her, though she loved the hunt almost as much as Sara. But as the true hostess of the weekend event, Elizabeth would respect her position and stay behind with the others.

No one knew that she would stay behind at the house as it was expected that she would be with the group as they jumped over fences and followed the hounds at breakneck speed through the rolling acres until the fox went to ground. William would ride and entertain from the saddle, but forced by etiquette, the ladies would simply socialise.

Then, after feasting on Cook's wonderful country ham and biscuits, gravy, grits, and grouse, the guests would saunter to their rooms or back to their homes to rest and nap before returning for the ball that evening. In the midst of her ponderings, Sara almost clapped with glee but controlled herself lest the horses think her crazy.

She rose from her hay bale and wrapped her coat around her tightly. The next few days were imperative that she be as alert as possible. She knew she must be by Elizabeth's side at every moment, especially following the ball.

She patted the noses sticking over the stall doors and tried to formulate her plan. Because William didn't know or understand what had happened to Elizabeth the night of the ball, she knew she had to be even more alert than she had ever been in the past. She had to watch for anything that seemed out of the ordinary and keep on her toes, no matter who might ask her to dance.

Having committed herself to her plan to save Elizabeth, she felt a renewed energy surge through her. On task, she whistled as she returned to the house where preparations for the big weekend were well under way and the clouds covered the sunshine in an ominous hue.

* * *

Excitement was the term of the day the following morning when Sara, Elizabeth, and Millie touched the bottom of the stairs for breakfast. Cook was singing in the kitchen as was her fashion, and the hired worked hoisted up a nine-foot-tall spruce tree, freshly cut from the adjoining pasture. The whole house rang with Christmas cheer, and the decorations were the icing on the cake.

Layers of white lace snowflakes danced from the tree by the time the decorating was complete. Amid laughter, the final touches of bright red ornaments were placed on the tree branches while William climbed to the top and added a beautiful angel. Houston and Thomas, always at hand, wrapped the tree with strung cranberries and candles that would be lit when the guests began arriving.

With the trimmings from the tree, wreaths were made for the front doors and the gates at the front of the drive. Dresses were pressed, suits were brushed, and collars were starched as everyone shifted into party mode.

By eight that night, a fine mist had begun to fall. Elizabeth and Sara giggled with their heads together, hoping the rain would turn to snow before the evening was finished. As they viewed the completed dressings of the house, Elizabeth sighed a deep breath as she took in the grandeur.

'Isn't this a lovely home?' she questioned to Sara, not really expecting a response but so enamored of the structure that she could barely believe her good fortune.

'I am astounded at how beautiful she is,' said Sara in agreement. 'I can't wait for the guests to get their first glimpse of it.'

It didn't take long for the first carriages to roll down the drive. The house was alight with gleaming candles in each window and chandeliers bright with the new electric power that had everyone in awe and envy.

Liveried footmen, hired from the local town, assisted the guests as they descended from their coaches or the new horseless carriages. What a sight it was to behold the advancements of technology all coming together in one setting!

People from around the state were in attendance at the soirée. Ladies were dressed in elegant gowns with gracious gloves and hats. Men were elegant in tailored suits befitting such an event, complete with bow ties and top hats. Photographers carrying the latest version of George Eastman's easy-to-use lightweight camera were on the scene to commemorate the social event of the season.

Though the jazz age hadn't yet graced the entrance of Crawdad, the musicians were lively as the played songs that lent themselves to ballroom dancing. Well-played selections from Irving Berlin and George M. Cohan's music tinkled in the drawing room where many guests stopped to chat with others about the probability of a war to end all wars, the changes in industry, Teddy Roosevelt's presidency, or Jack London's latest novel, *The Call of the Wild.*

Ladies discussed the latest fashions where skirts, called hobble skirts, measure over a yard in material and sported not only a slit to the knee but also shorter hemlines with the necessity of stepping into and out of the automobile. Their high-buttoned shoes still reminded them of the former days, though often, many opted for slippers instead. Above all, the fashionable elite were each doing their best to out-dress their friends.

Hairstyles had changed dramatically, at least to Elizabeth's way of thinking, since the turn of the century. Fashionable ladies had always worn elaborate chignons, upswept hair with lengths intertwined with curls, or just ole-fashioned buns. On this night, those in the know were bedecked with trendy bobs and other short cuts covered by hats that were often larger than life. Thankfully, per Sara's way of thinking, these were not plentiful!

As she slowly ambled from one room to the next, Sara was taken with the wide variety of costumes those in attendance chose to wear. She was also intrigued by their choices of conversation. One heavily bearded man in grey was harshly condemning the overall lack of qualified typewriter secretaries while the woman in a blue bustle was loudly proclaiming the wonders of author Owen Wister and his books *The Virginian* and *Lady Baltimore.*

Sara had read the latter book and delighted in the author's tale of a Northerner who visits the one-time aristocrats of the South following the Civil War and Reconstruction Era. It suddenly dawned on her that those days were relatively close at hand, considering the century that divided it from the world in which she had been reared. She had never formed a true idea of that period of time, but now, living among many who had served in the Northern or Southern armies, she had a different prospective of what really was lost in the battles that claimed lives and homes.

In the corner of the room, she found Samuel and two gentlemen in conversation. She strolled over the carpets to their side of the room and stood silently behind the trio to gain hearing of their conversation.

'It's not worth the cost, I tell you!' Samuel adamantly said. 'I am not willing to risk lives for something that should have been mine in the beginning!'

The tall, thin, and balding man to his right objected. 'You are not seeing the real picture here, brother. You have to look with your head and not your heart in this situation. We must have the money and the land if we are to build the academy to successfully train our young men in the skills necessary for survival.'

Samuel shook his head negatively and leaned closer to the men before saying, 'I will not risk my friends just for a possibility of what could come. You know as well as I do that the possibility of war is on the horizon. One false step, and we lose everything we've worked so hard to build.'

The second man, on Samuel's left, finally spoke. His voice was gravelly and gruff, sounding like the bass of the newly popularised barbershop quartets.

'The reason passion here, gentlemen, is not one of money or of property. It is one of power. With the erection of the academy's first walls comes the potential of bringing the South back to a reign of power. It is the twentieth century after all. Any gains that we can make is a step towards the declaration of the South's vast potential in both the agricultural field and the new develops we are seeing in the industry standard.'

'All the rhetoric is heroic only in speech,' Samuel debated. 'I truly believe in the South of yesteryear, but in my brain, I understand that South, its culture, and its complete way of life is gone forever. It is time to move forward with the world. You must embrace it, or the academy will never succeed.'

One man huffed at Samuel's words, but the other, the gruff-voiced man, remained silent. Gradually they changed the topic of conversation and soon ended it all together. Samuel was left standing alone. As Sara watched the man in grey capture some other poor soul in conversation, she turned and tapped Samuel on the shoulder.

'Why, here you are Samuel. I've been wondering if you'd like to dance with me tonight.' Sara purred the question even though she already knew the answer.

'Not tonight, Sara. I have a lot on my mind and many things I must take care of before it is over. Why don't you see if you can find Houston or Thomas or even William to entertain you?'

He never looked at her but continued to stare into his glass of whiskey. Then he turned and walked away from her as if she was a mere child he was indulging. She watched him stride from the room, bumping into a guest or two as he went. Soon he was out the front door and away from her view. She thought about following him to see what was so important in his night's events, but decided instead to find Elizabeth and stay close to her.

As she stepped from the room and back into the melee of guests and dancing couples, Thomas grabbed her by her unharmed arm and spun her around.

'You are looking much too serious, Sara! What you need is to have a good reel! Are you up for it?'

'I would love to reel, Thomas, if you think you can handle the dance,' she challenged. 'Perhaps you need to fetch William to handle me as a partner.'

Thomas looked into her eyes and grinned at the notion of Sara being a challenge! 'Are you mad? I can handle it with great grace, m'lady! Shall we?'

Laughing, the two of them contained themselves enough to walk with dignity into the ballroom and join the other dancers already in the heat of the dance. The reel was fun and energetic, taking no time to be caught completely by the rhythms and movements. As partners changed, Sara chose to stand in the circle of a group of dancers and perform the footsteps so as to keep her healing arm from risk. Before she knew it, several songs had been played and enjoyed by those enjoying the dance, and it was time for dinner to be served.

The gaslights danced in illumination for the guests as they entered the dining room where wonderful aromas watered palates. Amid all the opulence, however, the greatest presence was the beauty of

Elizabeth. She was regal. Though tiny in her frame, she stood with the grace of a queen.

Yet for all her elegance, her warmth greeted guests before they reached her outstretched hand as they entered the dining salon. Her face glowed with the happiness her laugh vocalised. Her sparkling eyes and high cheekbones would have won her Hollywood fame despite the fact that she didn't even reach her handsome husband's shoulders.

William matched her in charm and appearance. He looked very much the part of the gentleman; it was obvious to the eye to see he was. Like a presidential gathering, people stood in line to greet the couple and share a laugh with them. The mirth was genuine, a feeling that came from within rather than outward for appearances' sake.

The tables were filled to overflowing with china, silver, candles, and drinks. Servants handled the dishes, and guests filled plates with pheasant, venison, and goose. The vegetables were perfectly cooked, and yeast rolls all but floated in air; they were so light. A beautiful chandelier hung above the table.

Following the dessert course, William stood at the head of the table, and striking his goblet with his fork, a sound so festive, he asked for the attention of friends and neighbours. Silence gripped the hall as all stopped to hear his words. It was expected that tonight, William Alexander Cooper would announce his entrance into the political world, and each wanted to be one of the first to hear the news.

'Ladies and gentlemen, our dearest friends and family, Elizabeth and I are quite honoured to have you with us on this merry occasion.' William looked at his wife with eyes that could only be described as adoring. He put his right arm around her waist as he held a just-filled champagne glass in his left, slightly raised.

'Tonight is a very special night. Not only is this the wonderful season of Christmas, my precious wife's favourite time of the year, but tonight is a landmark for two delightful reasons.'

Again, William paused to let the mumblings of the room quiet.

'As many of you have already suspected, tonight I would like to invite each of you to join Elizabeth and me on a very exciting journey. Tonight, we embark on the pleasurable and challenging road of politics as I formerly announce my intentions of running for the Senate seat that Mr Albrighton will relinquish with his retirement next May. I invite each of you to participate in my campaign for this position because it is not just a job I undertake, but one we as citizens of this great nation should personally be responsible for by voting.'

A great cheer went up around the room. William could charm even an enemy into his corner, and he already had this room in his pocket. Many had speculated he would run for the elderly statesman's seat, so the surprise wasn't great, but the rumour simply solidified. Still, all were pleased that the young and already successful man would throw his hat into the ring.

'The announcement will hit the newspapers tomorrow morning as the letter of intention had to be filed by today. Elizabeth and I wanted to share it with you first.'

Again the applause rose as William leaned down and kissed his wife's cheek. She beamed up at him, and he squeezed her in tighter to his side. He once again extended his glass and the room was again silent.

'The other announcement we'd like to make is even more important to me. Ladies and gentlemen, I propose a toast to my beautiful wife, who is the apple of my eye and the song in my heart. Today Elizabeth has made me the happiest man in the world for she has told me we are expecting our first child.'

His words were received with gasps of delight and smiles all around. He leaned down and said something in her ear only she was aware of, and she too smiled more brightly than before.

A gentleman in the rear of the room rose and, lifting his glass, toasted the young couple's success and happiness. All joined the toast with enthusiastic response, and many rushed to hug the lady of the manor with congratulations.

William never left her side. He danced with her following the meal and was seen kissing her in the moonlight on the veranda as they stepped out for fresh air. Like charmed royalty, this couple had hitched their wagon to a moon, one guest commented, and away they had sailed.

For Sara, it was like revisiting a movie she had watched over and over. She was thrilled for William and Elizabeth, but silently her nerves were on high alert for any danger that might be forthcoming. Houston offered her his arm for a dance, and because she could keep her eyes on William and Elizabeth, she agreed. However, the thrill she enjoyed with his arms around her shoulders and waist was hers alone to enjoy.

Throughout the remainder of the evening, Samuel never returned. Sara, likewise, never saw either of the other men. Her curiosity was bursting by the time she and Houston stepped outside for some cool air and a cup of warm cider. She wondered if Houston knew the circumstances, and finally, she let the cat out of the bag and asked.

'Houston, Samuel hasn't been himself lately. Do you know what is troubling him?'

'Well, umm, Sara…'

'You can be honest with me, Houston. Neither my feelings nor my pride can be hurt by him any more than they already have been. Please, can you shed some light on it all?'

Houston, for such a tall and erect, not to mention handsome, man, shuffled his feet with a tied tongue. Finally he cleared his throat and began.

'Sara, you know I would never intentionally hurt you, so what I am going to tell you is not of my choosing but your curious self.'

He waited for Sara to nod her understanding before continuing.

'Samuel is running with a crowd of men who are rather rebellious in the truest sense of the word. He urges them to caution, but they are high-strung and insistent on getting what they think they deserve or once owned, no matter what happens. Thomas and I found this out yesterday when we came upon him in the barn. He was looking for some kind of papers that he said belonged to him.'

He paused, and Sara once again nodded in understanding. This was what she already knew, other than the papers report.

'We confronted him and asked his intentions. He told us part of William's property was his or once was supposed to be his. At any rate, he wanted the deed to that part of the property and was intent on finding it. We knew he was half-mad if for no other reason than he was searching for something of importance in the barn.

'He told us that we were all fools for following in William's footsteps, and he knew how to take himself to a higher level than we'd ever dreamed. The property would give him the needed leverage to buy his way into a group of men that were going to bring the South back to her feet.'

Sara gasped, not because of what he told her, but because the pieces were falling into place with the conversation that she had heard earlier.

Houston took the gasp as an expression of her shock and took her hand in his. 'I knew this would be hard for you. I'm sorry. May I continue?'

Again, Sara nodded in the affirmative and urged him to continue.

'During the conversation, Samuel admitted that he has no love for you and no intentions to marry you. He wants only to leave the area and begin a new life of his speculated well-being…'

Again, Sara gasped, this time in shock at the words she was hearing. But Houston carried on, not missing a beat.

'So I asked him if I could pursue you with the intention of marriage, if you should agree.'

Sara's gasp turned into a squeal, as unladylike a squeal as anyone could have ever heard if there was anyone nearby to do that hearing.

'Why, Houston, you flatter me. I am at once relieved to be shed of Samuel's false attention and thrilled to be so honoured by your intentions. That's the best Christmas gift ever!'

Standing on her tiptoes, Sara hugged the man who was, in one hand, saving her reputation and allowing her to ruin it in his arms.

'Sara, you are cold. We should go inside. I do promise to take care of you, and at the proper time, I will speak to William about your hand in marriage, if you are willing to wed me. But your Christmas present is inside under the tree. Shall we?'

Taking her elbow, he escorted her inside where other guests were opening presents and singing

Christmas carols. He left her standing beside Elizabeth and William as he slipped to the tree to retrieve her package.

William caught his eye, and he also gathered other presents clustered together.

'Oh, Houston is a Father Christmas tonight, is he?' Elizabeth giggled as he helped her sit in a chair and placed a large package on the floor beside her. Likewise he handed William a gift from his bride before escorting Sara to a spot that was somewhat empty to open their gifts and trying to find Thomas to give him a token from the hosts.

'To our future happiness my dear,' Houston said, presenting her a package.

'Well, open yours first,' Sara implored, although she was near to bursting with the excitement of her own.

'Okay, I will.' He grinned broadly as he looked lovingly into her eyes for the first time in public. 'What can it be? A rock? A new pair of gloves? What?'

'Open it,' she sang in response.

Inside the lovely wrappings, Houston gently uncovered a beautiful scarf that Sara had knitted for him. In addition, a lovely knife was tucked into the scarf.

'How did you know that I needed a scarf? Could it be because you used my last one on the snowman we made?'

But Sara didn't answer. She was gazing at him with all the love she felt. She shyly grinned at him before tearing into her present.

A white box lay underneath the wrappings of a beautiful cloth. She held the cloth up and looked closely at it. It was delicate and rich with a design that was mesmerizing.

'It is from India,' he said. 'It is a promise cloth that a man gives to a woman when he cherishes her heart. But look inside the box.'

Sara looked at him to help her as she struggled to hold the box with one hand and open it at the same time. He took it from her and held it before her allowing her full access to her prize.

Slowly she pulled the top off the bottom to find another piece of cloth, similar to the first, wrapped around a bulky object. With a giggle, she removed it from the box and carefully let the cloth drop back into the small compartment.

There in her hands was a tiny stuffed animal. It was made of brown cloth that resembled fur and had buttons for a nose and eyes. For anyone else standing in the room, Sara was sure the gift would seem inappropriate for a young woman who, after all, wasn't a child.

But Sara squealed for the second time that evening with delight. 'I can't believe it! An original teddy bear! I love it!'

Again she embraced him in her warm hug and clung to him, laughter still pealing from her lips.

'I'm glad you like it,' Houston whispered as he bent forward to hold her to him briefly. 'I always want to make you happy, as happy and safe as William makes Elizabeth.'

At his words, a cold chill crept up Sara's spine in an ominous warning.

Chapter 14

Amid much fanfare and shouted Christmas greetings, the party was over, and the guests retired either upstairs or to their own nearby homes. Sara strolled arm in arm with Houston into the parlour, picking up remnants of paper wrappings and ribbons along the way to the settee. She was so happy, yet she was also leery of the evening to come. If she had understood William correctly when he described the scene to her months ago, he and Elizabeth would retire to bed, but she would leave the bedroom and somehow go on a late-night ride that would leave her fatally injured in the pasture.

The questions of why and who remained unanswered until this day. While this was important to find out, Sara knew the real reason for her unease was how to stop Elizabeth's fateful journey down the stairs and out the door.

Houston was whispering something in her ear, but she was too engrossed in her own thoughts to hear him. Suddenly he reached around and kissed her, square on the lips! She had never been kissed before, except for stolen pecks from the choir boy at St Peters, and that couldn't really count, could it?

She was breathless and brainless as the kiss continued. She closed her eyes and reveled in the loving manner in which Houston held her and made her feel so special. What more could a girl ask for… except to be transported back into her own time and world with Elizabeth saved and all ending happily ever after!

'Hmm,' she heard herself murmur before he lifted his head and looked her in the eye.

'I can't wait to marry you, Sara,' he said with halted breath. 'I have wanted to tell you that for ages and never thought I would be able to do so.'

She smiled warmly back at him and knew that she would spend her life in happiness, regardless of whether she ever got back home or not. Houston made her, the old Sara, very happy.

'Excuse us,' William said from the doorway as he approached the young couple. 'Elizabeth and I are turning in for the night and wanted to tell you both how happy we are for you. Houston, shall we talk in the library for a moment.'

William smiled at Sara, and Houston squeezed her hand before leaving. She knew that now was her moment to convince Elizabeth to stay put this evening. No trips to the kitchen, the barn, or even the doorway to her room.

Sara glanced around the entry hall, but Elizabeth was nowhere in sight. She hiked up her skirt as high as she dared and raced up the staircase, slowing only when she came to the master suite. Timidly, she knocked on the door and waited for an answer.

None came. Frantically, she retraced her steps and was just walking into the parlour when the library door could be heard opening and a giggling Elizabeth emerged. She made a beeline to the parlour and, finding Sara, gave her an enormous hug before collapsing onto the settee beside her.

'I am so happy for you and Houston, my dear! Yours will be the wedding of the decade. We should plan it for the late spring so that all the roses around the house will be in bloom. Oh, what a beautiful bride you will make!'

Sara took both of Elizabeth's hands and, with a great deal of urgency, looked her straight in the eyes. 'Elizabeth, listen to me. Yes, I am terribly happy with Houston's declaration of love. Thrilled, in fact, but something is more pressing than late spring weddings at the moment.'

When Sara was certain she had Elizabeth's undivided attention, she continued. 'There are rumours about that someone may wish you or William harm. In fact, those rumours are very clear that tonight is the night when mischief could bring danger to you or to William. Please, whatever you do, when you go to bed, don't leave your chamber. Do you understand? It is imperative to your welfare that you heed my words.'

Elizabeth looked at first as though scared to death. Her face paled and her eyes were wide. Then, just as suddenly, she grinned as if she'd just heard the funniest joke. 'Sara, what are you ranting about, dear? No one is going to harm me or William. I fear you are just overwrought about the news you heard tonight from William and the lovely way your life has turned with Houston.'

'I am not overwrought, anxious, or mad!' Sara said earnestly. 'What I am is concerned for your very life! I am so concerned that I wish I could watch over you all night, but that is what William is for, I suppose. I just want you to promise me that for no reason will you leave you bedchamber.'

'It seems quite silly, but yes, I will indulge you. In fact, I do wish William would come along because I am so tired. My feet may resign my body and leave if he doesn't come along soon.' Elizabeth took Sara's hands again and squeezed them. Hers were cold to the touch, and Sara was once again worried about her welfare.

'You seem chilly, Elizabeth. Do you need a shawl? I'll fetch it for you.'

'No, I am perfectly fine. In fact, I am going to the kitchen to get some water, and then I am taking myself up the stairs to bed. You will have to tell William that I have given up waiting for him and the happy Mr Houston.'

Sara jumped from the settee. 'I will get you some water, Elizabeth. You just rest here.'

She fairly ran into the hallway and the kitchen for the water; so worried she was over whatever catastrophe might take place. Sara reached for the cabinet door, standing on tiptoes, and grabbed a glass from the shelf. As she regained her footing and moved towards the sink for the water, a burly arm grabbed her from behind and jerked her out the door and onto the porch.

The water glass fell from her hands with a scattering crash as Sara was pushed down the steps and into the yard.

The cold air hit her immediately and forced her brain into overdrive. Was this what Elizabeth had endured all those years ago when she was left for dead? Would she be a victim of the same fate? Or would she be a substitute for Elizabeth and be the one found in the moonlight?

Slung over her assailants' shoulder, Sara's head bounced against his back while she tried to gain momentum in hitting him with her fists. She kicked him in the chest with her legs while pounding him with her hands. He ignored her and kept striding towards the stables. He splashed in puddles of water, and mud splattered onto her face. Still she kept fighting.

'This one's a feisty one, boss,' the man said when he finally came to a stop. 'She's a kickin' and gougin' like nobody's business.'

'Just drop her there,' said a familiar voice behind Sara. 'Put her here in this stall and lock it. She'll settle down sooner or later.'

Sara listened carefully for any clue as to who the man was. She knew that she couldn't protect

Elizabeth and William if she didn't do something before the door was locked.

'Argh!' she began to wail. 'Argh!'

'What's wrong with her, boss?' the man asked before dropping her onto the hay-strewn floor. 'What's she going on about now?'

'Just leave her there, and don't waste time thinking about her childish antics. Now go!'

The stocky man dropped Sara to the floor and scooted out of the stall. In his haste, he neglected to lock the door behind him, if he even thought about it again.

In the darkness, Sara listened to the men's conversation in the aisle of the barn. At least two men were there, talking with the 'boss' who was giving them directions on where to walk, count, and dig. She was so curious she almost fell against the open door, which would have pushed it open into the hallway.

Instead she gently pushed it open just mere inches, just enough to stick an eye into the aisle to see if she could identify the people talking. She peeped out, but all she could see was a sack of grain and a stack of hay. She wondered why Joseph hadn't put it all into the feed shed like he normally would, but perhaps the party or the holiday had left his brain at home this morning.

Knowing the men had to be on the other side of the feed room, she duckwalked out the door of the stall and to the edge of the haystack. She held her breath so as not to be heard as she slowly glanced around the bales.

All she could see were the men's backs. They all stood in a semicircle, looking at a paper that one man held spread in front of them. The man holding what might be a map was dressed in formal garb as though he had been present at the party. Of the other two men, one was tall and balding while the other man was short and dirty with mud splashed across the back of his shirt and pants.

Well, I know who took me, she thought to herself as she looked at the evidence before her. But rather than focusing on that, she looked again at the man in the tux, trying to guess who he was.

'Boss, if we're gonna do this tonight, we'd better get at it. There's no sense in getting caught before we ever get stared.

'Did you leave the note like I told you to?' boss asked.

'Yes, I did,' said Mudpie Man, as Sara started to call him. 'I left a note on the kitchen table.'

'Good work, Gallaway,' the boss praised him. 'But I need you to stay close by the house so you can report to me what is happening now that the message is clear. We will trade Elizabeth for the burl wood document box from William's library in about an hour. In fact, if it's not at the designated area in forty minutes, Mrs Elizabeth dies!'

Sara's heart raced, and her breath caught in her throat. *The men are planning on killing Elizabeth, just like I thought!* her mind cried, but what could she do to protect her if she was here in the barn?

The men still stood with their backs to her, but the man had folded the paper and was pointing to some things in the tack room. He seemed to be directing the men to take supplies and be ready to ride to a place where he said he stored food and clothes for them.

Sara watched his body language. The way he held his arms was so familiar, but she couldn't place who it was. The man who had been completely silent nodded his head at something the boss was saying.

'Just leave her in the stall until we get the box of documents, or we have to take her with us. William will send the money and the deeds, just you wait. He'll deliver them himself once he reads that note and knows we have his precious wife!'

The men chuckled and slapped each other on the back as Sara waddled back into the stall and quietly closed the door.

Obviously the man who took her thought he had Elizabeth! While that was a relief in many ways to Sara's way of thinking, it was also problematic for her! She had to escape and still be able to keep Elizabeth safe and William's property secure.

'Gallaway, take Hensen to the back door of the house and leave him. He doesn't know the way. Once you leave him, report back to me. Now, get!'

Neither Gallaway nor Hensen seemed to be the sharpest tack in the box, so it didn't surprise Sara at all to hear the boss complain about their speed in leaving the barn. She sat in the corner with ears alert to hear anything that might be said or indication that the boss was leaving the stable as well.

She felt rather than heard his footsteps as he stopped next to the stall. She wanted to hold her breath in fear, but logic wouldn't allow it. She took a deep breath instead, and that was when she knew who the man was. She could smell his cologne, a bay rum that always irritated her nose.

But it couldn't be! How could he betray his friends like this! No! She refused to believe that the boss was someone she knew. Rather, she would force herself to believe it was just a case of the same smelly cologne used by anyone rather than him.

She heard someone outside the far stable door say something, and the boss started in that direction. Sara stood against the stall wall as closely as she could and slid along the walls to reach the stall door. Peeping through the crack, she willed herself to be completely silent as she pushed the door ajar the tiniest of inches for the second time so that she could see down the hallway.

A lantern sat on a hay bale, and momentarily, it blocked her view until her sight adjusted to the glow. Instead of helping her see, the light unfortunately prevented her vision. Moving back to her previous position, she carefully moved the lantern to another hay bale, but just as she did, the boss turned, as if knowing someone was there.

'Hey!' he hollered as he began running down the hallway.

With fight-or-flight adrenaline pulsing through her veins, Sara ran as fast as she could in her boots, throwing open the back door and racing for the closest protection she could find: the dog kennel.

As she jerked the door open and burst into the dogs' labyrinth, growls from every corner erupted. She had no idea which dog was lying where, so she randomly called names as she would on the hunt trail.

'Dandy, Dodger, Dobson,' she called, knowing the *D* list names of the foxhounds by heart. Each young whelped by Diana was named with a *D* name as well. The same was true of Agatha's litter; the offspring would be named with an *A* name such as Abigail or Angus.

A wet nose nuzzled her hand, and she patted a head then two. Suddenly the whole kennel was around her, except for those who were older or nursing young. Those dogs would be in a separate area.

'Hello, friends,' Sara crooned to the dogs, trying with all her might to remain calm and not upset the dogs. She felt her way to the ledge that allowed the dogs to sleep up off the ground and carefully sat among her four-legged buddies. She continued to rub backs and scratch ears, waiting for the other shoe to fall and be found by the boss and his men. The action served to keep the dogs quiet as well as steady her shaking nerves.

Just when she thought she was safe, the door jerked open, and growls deep in the throats of over forty dogs began, low and ominous, erupting into sharp, loud barks that took the dogs away from her and closer to those trying to get inside the kennel.

'Ugh!' a voice rose above the melee. 'Help! Boss!'

The dogs barked louder and, with an opportunity to run from the enclosed shelter, lunged at the door and men blocking their way. Screams of fright rose from those outside, and if Sara hadn't been so scared, she would have laughed at the men's terror of such gentle hounds. She heard a dog whine and another yelp, and suddenly, her safety was the last thing on her mind as she burst through the door to rescue the animals.

In turn, they began ripping and biting at the men in front of them. Quite a ruckus was raised, and lights began pouring from the house into the pasture. Sara was screaming at the men to leave the hounds alone, and the hounds were barking and growling as if to concur with her orders.

Against the moonlit sky, the darkness was as black as pitch, but somehow people were running everywhere. Arms circled around her waist as she struggled to get away. Dogs jumped and nipped at unknown and unwelcome visitors who refused to give up the fight they had embraced.

A sudden sound of a gun ripped through the darkness, and both dogs and humans stood briefly in wonderment before racing in various directions for safety. A loud *gruff* was heard as the stocky man known as Gallaway tripped and slid head first into a tree. He was quickly grabbed and held securely as he was taken away for questioning.

'It's okay! I'm just here to help,' Thomas screamed as someone grabbed onto his shoulder and turned him to face them. 'I ran out here when I heard the dogs. I knew something must be wrong for there to be such as fuss.'

'That is not true!' Sara screamed in reply. 'He is the one who told that other man to take me and to be prepared to kill me if William didn't bring or send the burl wood document box!'

William walked up to face Thomas and grabbed him around the neck. 'Is that true, dear Thomas? Did you have your men take Sara?'

'No! I would do no such thing, William. On my honour as a gentleman, I never sent anyone to harm Sara.'

'Of course you didn't,' Sara said as she drew near the men with Houston at her side. 'You thought that I was Elizabeth. You wanted to use her as bait for whatever it is in that box that you want. How could you, Thomas? How could you want to hurt your friends? Only a coward of the worst kind would ever harm someone else.'

With each word she spoke, Sara's adrenaline crashed until she was sobbing. She found herself sitting on the ground with arms around her knees, and she released the fear for Elizabeth, for herself, and the hounds as it slowly seeped away.

'Thomas, I think you have a lot of explaining to do regarding your actions and your devious plans, which thankfully Sara rescued us all from facing. I want to know why you would do this, and then I want you out of our home and our lives. I no longer call you friend or brother!' William said with heart-felt vehemence.

With arms securely held by stable hands, Thomas was led inside and locked in the food pantry until the sheriff and his men arrived.

'Let's get you inside, my dear,' Houston said as he picked up Sara and carried her to the house. Her clothes were filthy and her shoes ruined from the wet ground, but she clung to Houston as if he was a life-line. Once inside and up the stairs, Grace took over immediately, and soon Sara was clean, warm, and ready for bed.

'I must see Elizabeth before I go to sleep, Grace,' she said. 'Is she in her room?'

'Yes, ma'am. I think she is. Shall I fetch her for you?'

'No, I will go to her. She's had enough of a fright tonight worrying about William, me, and her dogs.'

She knocked gently at the door and was immediately admitted by Elizabeth herself, who wrapped her arms around Sara and held her tightly. 'Thank heavens, you're safe! What a fright you must have had and because of Thomas of all people! I am so sorry you had that experience in the dark and cold, but I am so thankful you are okay.'

Both women had tears of relief running down their face but quickly reassured the other that she was safe.

'This plot was meant for you, Elizabeth,' said whispered. 'I don't know what the whole story is, but you were to be the bait to bring William to his senses if he wouldn't give up some document. I am so glad you listened to me and didn't leave the house tonight.'

'After this, I don't think I'll be venturing out after dark again,' Elizabeth said. 'When I think of all William and I could have lost tonight...including you...I am delighted for once I kept myself where I was supposed to be instead of being a curious cat!'

Laughing, the ladies hugged each other again, and saying good night, Sara returned to her room. She crawled into bed feeling exhausted on more levels than she could name, but knowing without a doubt that Elizabeth and she were safe, at least until morning.

She lay still in the bed and listened to William's footsteps on the stairs. She knew he was now skillfully in charge of taking care of Elizabeth, and with the long day finally behind her, Sara slept like a baby.

Chapter 15

Because the evening had lasted well into the morning, the breakfast that was planned was delayed until after luncheon hours. Added with the wonderful aromas of leftover ham and turkey, various vegetables, and lots of desserts, the experience was leisurely and lasted for most of the afternoon.

No one wanted the time spent together to end, especially after the diabolical event that could have been the result of last night's chaos. William was silent as he sat at the head of the table and allowed his guests to speculate on all the mystery surrounding Thomas and the attempted kidnapping.

Once the party had broken and fond farewells were said to their remaining guests as they took their leave and a hot cup of tea, William, Elizabeth, Sara, and Houston sat in the parlour and relaxed. Sara noticed that someone had replaced a large arrangement with a beautiful Victrola that Elizabeth had received from William for Christmas. She recognised it immediately as the one that still remained in the parlour at Elizabeth's Place.

It struck Sara as she comfortably sat next to Houston that so many things were different this morning as opposed to the mornings of the past few weeks. No longer was there the sense of danger hanging over her head. There was no need to protect, but yet she wondered why she hadn't been transported back into the twenty-first century if the threat to Elizabeth was indeed over. Would she ever go back, or would she spend the rest of her life here in this age?

A knock at the front door brought the sheriff and his deputy to the home, and William and Houston excused themselves from the women to discuss issues with the officials. The door to the library was firmly closed, and Elizabeth hummed softly under her breath until she was sure no one could hear her.

'Sara, something isn't right about Thomas and his shenanigans last night,' Elizabeth confided. 'William is very confused and concerned with this turn of events because it makes no sense to him either. The burl box only contains a few letters, but nothing of any importance to Thomas. There is nothing there that would be valuable to him. Certainly not anything that would necessitate harming you or me to get his way.

'Did he say anything to anyone that would give us a hint of what he was thinking? Was there anyone's name mentioned that he might have been working with in this affair? William is dumbstruck to think that Thomas is truly a bad person, but the facts seem to colour him in just that light.'

Sara could see the disappointment and hurt in Elizabeth's face when she spoke of Thomas. He had been a dear friend for many years, and the why of this was not only confusing, it was devastating as well. Thinking carefully back through the time she was held captive, Sara could only think of the way the other two men had called Thomas 'boss' over and again. She related this to Elizabeth.

'They called him Boss each time they referred to him. Never did they say his name. For the longest time, I couldn't place why he was familiar. Of course, I couldn't see his face because he was standing with his back to me,' Sara said. 'I do remember him calling the one man Gallaway, but I'd never heard of him before. He was the shorter man.

'And he had a map or a large piece of paper like the size of a map. He was showing the men items on the drawing and said something about having food and provisions stored somewhere that they were going to stay for a while once William gave them the box.'

'Were you terribly scared, dear?' Elizabeth asked in a whisper.

Sara almost laughed. 'No, actually, I wasn't frightened by them. I was curious and perhaps a bit angry because Gallaway ruined my dress, but my thoughts were for you and William. I knew I had to get away from them because I had to be able to save you.'

The voices of the men leaving the library as they bid each other goodbye were heard in the hallway, and William and Houston returned to Elizabeth and Sara.

'Well, that was very enlightening,' said William with a sarcastic chuckle. 'It would seem that our Mr Thomas wasn't Thomas at all. All these years he has been hiding behind a name that wasn't his.

'Years ago, Thomas had an uncle who lived near Crawdad. It seems the man was a bit baffled by the way his life had turned, what with the war and all, and he tried to establish himself in the area as an investor. He took a great deal of money from folks in and around these counties and settled in Gladesville in an attempt to become legitimate once again.'

'What does this have to do with you, William?' Elizabeth asked, interrupting him.

'Well, no one is really sure, but according to the sheriff, the uncle and this supposed Thomas man were partners of sorts. The uncle died years ago, but he hid his money somewhere in the area, and for whatever reason, it was imagined by Thomas to be here, or at least, near here.'

'So what did he intend to do?' Sara queried. 'Was he going to dig up the entire farm to find something that might not even exist?'

Houston took her hand and answered. 'According to the man named Gallaway, he was to follow a map that Thomas had and lay stakes to mark spots along the property. Then, one by one, he would dig in those spots. But he never got around to it because the map went missing several weeks ago.

'Thomas assumed that William had the map and the letters from the uncle. He knew that if William had found it, he would know the property well enough to find the points of interest and, thereby, the fortune.'

'So that's what he thought was in the box?' Sara asked.

'Well, he wasn't sure, but he had seen William sort through the items in the box often enough over a period of time that he knew that was where many important items were stored. He never considered that the box was too small to store a map as large as a property map.'

'But he had something that was as large as a map last night,' Sara said. 'Was it the real map? And if so, how did he get it back?'

William stood from his chair and crossed the room to the fireplace. He leaned his arm on the mantel and looked into the flames.

'He had tried to recreate the map, but he couldn't remember where many of the *X* spots were. That's why he felt that he had to obtain both the deed of the property and the map he thought I had. By having the deed, he would have time to dig and find the treasure he felt was here. Of course, he never thought about how he would remove us from the premises. In fact, he never thought clearly about almost anything, it seems.'

'But when did Thomas decide that he was going to do this to you, William?' Elizabeth's question hung in the air between all of them for several moments before William answered.

'We have been friends for many years, first at the academy and then in business ventures. I don't know when Thomas turned from good to bad, or if he always was, and his planning just all fell together. He always seemed so sincere. But for whatever reason that he might choose, it would appear that the apple didn't fall far from the family tree of evil intentions.'

'Did anyone mention Samuel? Was he involved in this scheme?' Sara muttered.

'No,' William stated matter-of-factly. 'I think that poor Samuel is just a man on a mission that even he doesn't understand. He wants to buy land for an academy he and some men are dreaming of, but I don't think that the outcome is going to be a positive one. Not in this area, anyway.

'He was perhaps hoping that Thomas could aid him in his search for funding and erecting of the building. But all Thomas was concerned about was his own dire need for money that was to be found on the farm.'

'So if he had acquired the farm, he would have hunted for this phantom treasure until he found it. And if he never did?' Elizabeth remarked.

'Perhaps he would have sold the farm and moved on to another endeavor,' William responded. 'The sheriff and his deputy still have him in custody and are trying to get answers out of him, but the real essence of the matter is greed. He wanted what his uncle had managed to steal from others. And he was prepared to use any means necessary to get to that end.'

'Then on top of that treasure,' Houston interjected, 'he had heard of the Thurman treasure. Folks have known that Mr Thurman was determined to hide and preserve what he could of the family heirlooms as the war raged on in the area. Some folks say that the location of the silver and money died with him, while others believe that once the Northern and Southern troops left the area for Atlanta that he retrieved it and put it back in the house.'

'So the possibility of there being a treasure is slim? Right?' Sara asked.

Houston tweaked her on the nose and grinned at her. 'Always the curious cat, aren't you, Sara?'

'Well, one should know what to expect if there could be danger or intrigue afoot!' She laughed as they all contemplated the possibility of treasure and hidden riches.

'The important thing is that everyone is safe,' announced Elizabeth as she took up her needlework and punched the thread through the delicate fabric.

'I would guess our adventures are, for the moment, over,' said William. 'I think that the rest of the holidays should be spent in peace and quiet. How about listening to your new gift, my love?'

William busied himself with the workings of the Victrola, and soon the sounds of music wafted through the house. Though the criminal was captured, the elements of intrigue were for Sara as scratchy as the album that played more and more slowly until William wound the handle once again.

'I still just don't understand how Thomas, or whatever his name really is, laid the plans for this colossal endeavor. He would have had to have known years ago about you and the property and his uncle and his dirty dealings. One little change over the years, and nothing like this would have been possible.'

'Sara, fate is a mighty fickle thing,' William surmised. 'Once he knew us and what our plans for the future were, he simply put two and two together with his uncle. From there it wasn't hard to be a part of our inner circle. He knew our dealings and ventures—was part of them in fact—so he was able to manipulate much of what he needed to happen to reality. He made his future work for him by ensnaring all of us into his life. The property, the money, and the legends all seemed to fall into place with his proposition to find his fortune. Perhaps his meddling with fate is his downfall.'

As the others talked and listened to the gramophone, Sara thought over William's words. Would her meddling in fate be her downfall? While she was certain that Elizabeth was still alive because of her meddling, she wondered if fate would come back to haunt her in later years?

She laid her head against Houston's shoulder and soon dozed off to sleep as the music refrains repeated over and over in her subconscious. Her mind drifted through the weeks that had passed. She wondered about her dogs left in another time, and she hoped they were safe. But in reality, she had to question if the dogs even existed. For that matter, if she ever returned to her future, would William still be a part of it, or would his life be complete in this time because Elizabeth was still alive this day? She couldn't bear to think about the possibility of living at Elizabeth's Place in the future without the companionship of William, but in saving Elizabeth, she probably had ensured herself a life without him.

As she dozed, she dreamed of horses and flowers on the property. She floated through laughter and times spent with her friends at the country store. Her mind played tricks with her as she built snowmen and made angels in the snow beside trees that in this time were just beginning to grow. At the same time, she had the thought of strawberry pies and wondered why that vision had played in her dreams.

Strawberry pies, strawberry pies…smashed strawberries and broken eggs…

Sara's eyes flew open, and she jerked abruptly on the settee. The burl wood document box still sat on the desk in the library at Elizabeth's Place. She had seen it there so many times, but she'd never taken the time to explore its holdings. Now she wondered if important papers were still held there. Could it be that clues to a possible treasure still existed in the house? Was Thomas truly on to something with his treasure hunt?

Sara knew that just last year, there were people exploring in the caves around the farm hunting for treasure. They too had been arrested and imprisoned for a variety of crimes, although trespassing on her property wasn't one of them. Now her curious nature was kicked into overdrive.

'William, may I ask what you do keep in your box on the desk? The one that Thomas wanted,' Sara said out of the blue to those in the room.

'Treasures, my dear Sara. I keep all the treasures of my life in that box.' William laughed. 'There is the knife my grandfather gave me and a pouch of tobacco that Elizabeth loves to smell. I do keep some letters in there, but there is no mysterious map of long-ago hidden pirate's gold! I hate to disappoint our cat!'

'I am curious about it, I must admit,' Sara said with a chuckle. 'I hope I haven't earned myself the name cat though. I was just wondering if the box is the safest place to put important documents.'

The recording stopped on the Victrola with a slow tempo. William relieved the needle from the record and returned to his seat near Elizabeth.

'Sara, if there is a treasure on this property, I think that I would have uncovered it, what with cropping and building. But if there is treasure here, I will leave the finding of it to some future generation. I have all the treasure I need right here.'

With that, he rose and took Elizabeth by the hand. He cranked the Victrola into play once again, and the couple waltzed around the parlour, laughing in the merriment of life.

Chapter 16

The weeks that passed following the exposure of Thomas were uneventful. The New Year came in with little excitement, and the weather turned dreary and cold. Finally the skies opened up and released snow in vast amounts, perfect for making snowmen and angels, to Sara's delight.

One morning in the midst of a perfectly clear day, Samuel rode up to the house with a renewed sense of self. He spoke to William for several long minutes before emerging from the library. Seeing Sara in the parlour, he knocked on the doorframe before entering. She smiled up at him and invited him to sit and have a cup of tea. He denied the pleasure of both, but congratulated her on her engagement to Houston with much delight.

'I hope you can understand why I couldn't see us as a couple,' he said to her. 'I knew that Houston loved you, had known for many years, but I just didn't know how to encourage him without seeming to harm you. I knew that I had made a commitment to the academy, and I wanted to see it to fruition.'

'And how is the school coming along?' Sara asked without a trace of resentment.

'Well,' he quietly said, 'it is coming along well. The board of directors has appointed me as headmaster, so I am assisting in much of the decision-making where the building is concerned. I hope that one day the school will be a success not only for the students but for the community as well.'

'You have my best wishes,' said Sara with a smile. 'What will you call the school?'

'The final name hasn't been decided because two of the board members want it named after one gentleman, while another group wishes it to honour another man. It will be an all boys' school, of course, specializing in a Latin Classics foundation. Personally, I'd like to see less classrooms and more outdoors studies and activities. The hills and history lends the school to that type of teaching.

'I was here to ask for William's support when the school opens. I would truly enjoy having a young Cooper in a class when he is old enough to attend. He, of course, pledged his contributions as well as moral support to the academy.'

'Well, it seems congratulations are in order all the way around then.' Sara beamed. 'Your success and the school's success can be shared by one and all.'

Samuel went on and on about the school to Sara, who offered a willing ear. He discussed the aspects of boarding school versus day school as well as how many dormitories would be necessary to house the young men and the amount of workers that would be needed to manage such a facility.

When he at long last seemed to run out of things to say, he took his leave. His step was light as he turned to the entry and left the house. Just as he opened the front door, the sun came out from behind the clouds and shone on his head.

To Sara, it was an omen of happy sailing for the man who had once seemed so discontent with the world. She smiled to herself as she once again glanced at patterns for dresses, knowing that spring would eventually arrive, and she would need a new trousseau for after the wedding.

Plans were already in full swing for the couple's big day. Set in late May, she knew the grounds around the house would be beautiful, and just the thought of the day made her pulse quicken. Several neighbours had offered to host parties for the bridal couple, but William and Elizabeth insisted on holding the first of them.

Sara knew deep inside that the reason was twofold. First, William and Elizabeth wanted to show the community just how much they loved the couple, but Sara also knew that Elizabeth wasn't going to retain her trim figure for many more months with the baby due in June. So many wonderful happenings occurring in just a matter of months!

Wonderful smells were whisking through the air, and Sara put her things aside to visit the kitchen. Cook was busy as always with the baking of bread and the making of cakes, her downtime in between meal preparation. She was vigorously beating eggs for a cake when Sara walked into the room, and she immediately told her to walk softly lest her cake falls that was in the oven.

Sara stood silently and watched the robust woman work.

'Cook? Would you teach me to cook and bake?'

'You? Cook and bake? What is up with you, sweet girl? Don't you think that Mr Houston will make certain you have kitchen help when you move to his home?'

Sara blushed. 'I'm certain he will, but I would truly enjoy learning the art of making his food. Would you teach me? Please.'

'Well, what's keeping your feet from moving? Get over here, and we can start with learning the basics of making meringue!'

The rest of the afternoon was spent with Sara assisting Cook in icing a cake, adding meringue to the pies, and even peeling potatoes. She learned the basics of making cornbread and battering chicken before Cook shooed her from the kitchen so that she could get dinner ready for the table.

Sara walked away feeling better about herself than she had in many days. She felt confident that she would be able to feed herself and Houston should the need or desire ever arise.

As she approached the staircase, a hauntingly familiar feeling floated over her. It was like a cold chill crept up her spine, just as it often had when she was living alone in the house. However, the man who often left that impression with her was not a ghost and therefore should not give off a ghostly feeling.

She climbed the stairs and then, on a whim, turned and traced her steps, ignoring the door to the parlour and heading to the library. It had become one of her favourite places when she had first arrived at Elizabeth's Place, and today, she needed a bit of home.

She opened the door and entered the dark room. Her feet knew the way well and took her to the large windows that stood along the northern side of the home. Throwing backing the curtain, she drew in a breath of home and relished in the weak sun flowing through the window.

She wandered through the room and pulled first one book then another from the shelves as she decided what to read. She finally chose a book of poems by John Keats and sat in her favourite chair to read the lyric context of 'Ode to a Nightingale,' though 'Bright Star' was one of her favourites.

It surprised her she chose Keats, an author who was passionate about his work and, though successful, died at such a young age of mercury poisoning that he had only a brief time to enjoy his earnings. She could relate to him in so many ways; it seemed that her life had just begun for her at Elizabeth's Place before she was thrown backwards in time to the original Elizabeth and William's home. How odd that she had rarely thought on the subject of her transferal from a modern reality to a passive yesteryear. The book fell to her lap, and her eyes closed in thought in the familiar surroundings. Here, she was at peace.

How long she was there, Sara did not know. She dreamed briefly of a sun-bathed meadow. She could hear the bellowing of the cows in the distance and feel the caress of the late afternoon wind. She felt the need to follow something, but she couldn't see anything to follow. More than anything, she felt the need to rest for she couldn't bring herself to make her eyes open.

She tried to recline and stretch out in the sun's warmth, but it had strangely disappeared. She tried to sit up, but her body wouldn't obey, and instead she found herself dreaming of yards and yards of thick molasses that held her feet and legs in its grasp.

Swirling, swirling dark clouds gathered at the edge of her sleep, and she knew she must escape before a storm drenched her. Her anxiety mounted and her heart raced as she remained trapped without a way of escape. In the distance, she could hear voices calling her name, over and over, each time with more urgency.

Suddenly the door banged against the wall, waking her from her troubled slumber.

'Oh, there you are!' Elizabeth said, relieved. 'It is time for dinner, and Cook said you had left her some time ago, but you weren't in your room.'

'I must have fallen asleep,' Sara said against a yawn. 'I'm sorry if I've kept you waiting. I will go quickly change and be right down.'

'Don't worry about changing tonight. It's just you and me for dinner as William and Houston are attending a meeting at the Capitol. They've been gone all day, but I guess you knew that.'

'Well, I knew they weren't here this afternoon, but I didn't have any idea where they had gone. Is it something of urgency that took them there?'

'No, it is just a regular meeting that goes hand in hand with being a magistrate and upcoming candidate for a political seat. Let's go in to dinner. Cook is waiting.'

Their meal and evening passed with relative peace despite Elizabeth's occupation with hummingbirds and how best to attract them in the spring. She carried on and on about the tiny rarely seen birds until Sara declared herself exhausted and bid her good night.

In her room, she took the book of poetry and tried to read, but the words kept blurring on the page, so she finally turned out her lamp and relaxed in the bed to think on many things regarding the wedding, the move to Houston's home, and the flowers she would plant for the spring. However, sleep quickly overcame all her ambitious thoughts, and she fell into the abyss of darkness.

Sometime during the night, Sara thought she heard talking outside her door. She roused herself enough to swing her legs to the floor and walk to the door, but when she got there, the hallway was empty, and no sound could be heard.

Odd, she thought to herself, how all these little bumps in the night were making her so anxious. That wasn't like her. She was a sound sleeper who awoke feeling restored and ready for a new day. All that seemed to have changed in recent months, and she rarely woke without a dull headache or a lagging feeling about her.

She once again curled up under the coverlet of the bed and dove back into sleep, and this time when the voices began, she listened closely to what was being said, though she couldn't see anyone talking.

'Can she hear us?' someone asked.

'They say people can hear when they're in comas,' another replied.

The conversation made no sense, so Sara immediately thought she must be eavesdropping on someone else's dream.

'Ridiculous!' her mind screamed at her, but just like it had begun, the voices were gone, and sleep overtook her tired brain.

She tossed back and forth in the arms of her dreams. She couldn't dislodge the thought of being at the wrong place or in the wrong time, but yet, none of it made sense to her. She struggled with the logic behind being in two time periods at once, and while she accepted it, her body taunted her and called her names for her thinking in general.

Long before dawn's light touched the grey sky, Sara rose and dressed. She added her heavy winter coat to her outfit, and carrying her boots in her hands so as to not wake the house, she tripped down the stairs and out the doors. Sitting on the cold steps of the porch, she hurriedly put her boots on her feet, pulled mittens on her hands, and walked briskly to the stables.

The nickering of the horses welcomed her as she stepped inside the warm barn. Curled on a hay bale, a small orange kitten lifted its sleepy head and purred at her as if to ask why she was disturbing her so early in the morning.

She petted each nose that emerged from the stall doors in greeting and then entered the tack room for a halter and a bridle. As she adjusted the straps to fit the gelding's face, she made quick work of taking him from the stall and rubbing him down before adding a saddle from the wall to his back.

Cinched and bridled, she took the bay beauty to the doorway of the stable and mounted him, giving him his head as he galloped out of the pasture. Sara thrilled at the cold air slapping her in the face as she breathed in deeply the icy breeze. The gelding pranced through his paces before Sara took him to the fence and soared over first one then the second coop. The pair flew through the air as hooves met ground, only to delicately take flight again.

Miles flew behind them as they raced from one field to the other, slowing only to cross the stream that criss-crossed the property multiple times. Finally she pulled her mount to a halt and watched the sun rise in the eastern sky, illuminating the horizon with fiery brilliance.

She patted the neck of the horse as they stood, him exhaling white puffs of steam into the cold atmosphere while she hugged the chill away from her freezing body. With a need to feel the wind again, she urged him into a canter and then a run, letting him pick the ground and the direction.

When the sun was bright enough to see the way through the trees of the growth around her, Sara guided him in the direction of the caves she knew were on the property. She debated about exploring them but decided the timing of the season wasn't in her favour should bears be resting and kept riding.

Following the tree line, she wove in and out of the birch trees, riding along the trunks of the century-old elms and chestnuts before turning towards a stand of hickory nut trees. Under the arms that reached for the sky, she dismounted and let the horse rest. She picked her way through the thick brush and carefully sought a place out of the wind to lean against a tree.

The ground looked very well-traveled in this area, which surprised her as deep in the woods as she felt they had journeyed. Markings were notched on the bigger trees whose bark stood out from the tree trunk, as if leaving a trapdoor for animals who wished to enter. She became so interested in the markings and notching on the trees that she wandered far inside the grove, and darkness soon reclaimed her.

How she wished she'd paid attention to where she was going. Not that she could be lost because the grove hadn't looked that deep. She would simply turn completely around and reverse her path. But after several minutes of walking, she discovered that retracing her steps was only simple if one left a bread-crumb trail, similar to Hansel and Gretel.

She walked for some time trying to find the way out, but instead felt that she was farther inside the grove than ever before. She decided to let her feet guide her rather than her brain and again began exploring the tree trunks around her.

Several trunks were scarred with X marks on their lower barks while still others contained an *A* on the branch closest to the ground. One after another, she followed the trees. Before she knew it, she was on the outskirts of the grove and in front of a rock wall. The wall ran to her left and right, following the lay of the land. It was obviously a livestock retention wall, much like a barbed wire fence that surrounded her property today. She realised that she was on the opposite side of the grove from where she had originally entered and began traipsing around the outside of the grove in order to find her horse.

Once collected, she mounted and urged him in the direction of the rock wall, wishing to explore the properties around them.

A bright refection hit her in the face about mid-way there. Curious as she was, she couldn't help but wonder what the sun was hitting as it rose farther in the sky. Determinedly, she rode in the direction, shielding her eyes to knock off some of the glare. When she reached the rock wall, the reflection was beaming, emitting warmth from its shine onto the earth.

Once again, she dismounted and dropped the reins as she concentrated on the shiny object just this side of the wall. She bent low to discover the source, only to find herself flying face first through the air and onto the ground.

She spit grass and dirt out of her mouth once her breath returned to her body and looked around her to make certain the horse was still where he was supposed to be. He was munching on what little grass showed through the patches of snow, not complaining about his early morning run.

She crawled on the ground, searching for the source of the shiny reflection but found nothing. She walked back to the horse, turned again towards the fence, and was hit full in the face with the bright reflection. That was when she noticed it came from the rock fence and not beside it.

She ran to the spot where she had seen the bright light and leaned into the fence so as to rest her weight against the rocks. She pushed and shoved to get to a narrow passage where a key stuck half in and half out of its rock fortress. She grabbed the key and pulled, her weight keeping her steady. Finally the wall released its prisoner, and she fell flat on her back in a big patch of crusty snow.

As she fell backwards, the horse walked forward, and the collision that ensued was as wet and muddy as it was harmful to Sara's head. When the gelding took a step backwards as she pounded onto the ground in front of him, his hoof grazed the side of her head, opening a wound that brought both stars and tears to her eyes.

She lay on the ground trying not to be sick for some time while the gelding nuzzled her shoulder as if to check on her condition. She sat up and took the reins, but when she tried to stand, her head swirled, and a blinding light made her hold her head in anguish. Sara dropped to her knees with the pain. Her final thought before she fainted was for the care of the horse, so with an awkward slap against his rump, she sent the horse flying home.

Wet, muddy, and bloody, Sara lay on the ground, unaware of her surroundings and even less aware of the cold that seeped into her body. The sun rose higher, but help didn't come. Not that Sara was aware of needing help or that there wasn't any to be found. Instead, grasping the key that had led her to her potential doom, she appeared more a bag of used clothing than a girl on the forest floor. She was protected by the outstretched arms of the hickory trees from the wind, but she didn't take notice of that either. Instead, she simply slept the sleep of the almost dead.

Chapter 17

Sara floated in limbo. At times she heard mechanical beeps and trills in the far corners of her mind; at other times, she heard birds singing in the overhead branches of the ancient trees. Sometimes she felt as if someone was touching her cheek while other times it was obviously just a wisp of wind as it breezed by her face.

In the lucid moments, Sara was aware that she was lying on the ground. It was hard beneath her and very uncomfortable on her back. She was often awake to the world around her, knowing when the sun was shining or when the night crept into the picture.

Always, there was the painful sensation of burning spasms up and down her legs and back. She continuously battled a headache that felt like small bombs exploding in her brain. Her eyes didn't want to open on her command, and her ears felt as if plugged with cotton packing. She wanted a drink of water but couldn't even tell anyone how thirsty she was.

And she was cold. So cold that she thought she would freeze. Sometimes she prayed that she would just drift into a deep sleep and never awaken so that the cold would leave her. If she could just find the coverlet, she knew she could pull it closer and get some relief of the icy fingers that embraced her.

On those rare moments, Sara would remember her glorious ride that morning. She would picture the beautiful sunrise once again and imagine herself soaring over the fences and riding through the pastureland. When those moments came, she wondered if anyone had missed her at breakfast this morning at Elizabeth's Place or if Elizabeth had slept in and hadn't yet discovered she was gone.

And what about Houston? Had he stopped to see her this morning? Did he know that her horse had returned to the stables without her? Or had the horse made it home yet? How long had she been here?

She tried valiantly to bend her knees up to her chest. There was no movement except what she imagined in her mind. Some insect buzzed by her nose, but she couldn't make her arms to move to swat it out of her way. And she really wanted to sleep. Her eyes were closed, but her mind was not functioning enough to wake up and move or lie still and rest.

There was no doubt about it—she was in limbo.

* * *

Though Sara was unaware of her circumstances, Houston had indeed stopped by to see her that morning and, finding her missing, had hurried to the stables to determine where she might have ridden. Once there, the groomsmen told him that the horse and tack were missing, but Sara was nowhere to be found.

He mounted his horse and, calling to William through the study windows, headed towards the back of the farm where the wildlife ran free at the early hours of the morning. He watched carefully for footprints, any indication of foul play that might be found in the thawing ground, but saw nothing.

The sun was high in the sky by the time he found the gelding wandering and eating the crunchy winter grass. He ground-tied him and went deeper into the tree line, hoping to find Sara wandering herself towards home.

While he couldn't imagine what she was thinking in riding so early in the morning, panic began to set in as the sun descended in the western sky. The temperatures were dropping, and he knew from the wind that had increased that another cold night was on the horizon for the family at Elizabeth's Place.

Deeper and deeper into the overgrown forest he rode, knowing in his heart that he should turn back and get more help to speed up the exploring but not wanting to leave in case he should miss her along the way.

He passed a stand of birch trees that, even in the winter, raised their lovely white arms to the sky. Leafless, one would think trees would be see-through, but it seemed he literally couldn't see the forest for all the underbrush and foliage growing there.

As he rounded the ridge along the farm that held the largest grove of hickory nut trees he'd ever seen, Houston pictured an autumn scene of picking up the nuts with Sara and then roasting them until they burst open. While he doubted her brave enough to enter the dense grove, he also knew that anywhere was fair game as to her location.

Houston dismounted and picked his way through the brambles and sticker bushes that captured his pants legs. He pushed his way past the thick sleeping growth of thorny blackberry vines and finally cut his way between the stand of hickories and English creeper. Where the once deep green leaves had grown under the summer sun, only prickly vines of brown clung to other trees and across the ground floor.

He turned to leave the area where the undergrowth was the thickest, but he couldn't get his jacket sleeve to release the tendrils of spiny stickers that kept him bound to the stick-tight bushes and prickly pears along the way. He was covered worse than a hound after a hard run through the woods.

Houston stood perfectly still and began to dislodge the long, spindly needles from his clothing. Though the needles couldn't hurt anyone, he didn't want to take a chance in bringing them home to find root. He knocked and brushed the offensive needles off his clothing and then his jacket before having to individually pick them from his gloves. As he picked, he walked around the small clearing and finally came across hoof prints and those of small boots.

He followed the trail that Sara unknowingly left behind, losing them momentarily only to find them again. Just as he was about to give up and turn in the other direction, he saw a bright spot of red and ran to it. There on the ground, half frozen from the melting pockets of snow, was Sara.

He said a prayer of thanksgiving as he bundled her to him. She didn't rouse from his touch, but he felt a pulse.

'How could one girl get into so much trouble?' he questioned aloud as he hoisted her into her arms and carried her out of the grove, making much better time than his approach through the trees.

Grabbing the reins of his horse, he laid Sara as carefully as possible over the saddle and mounted. Holding her to him, he kicked his steed into a trot and returned to the area where he had ground-tied her horse. He picked up the reins in one quick movement, startling the animal that obediently followed behind him as they made tracks back to Elizabeth's Place.

* * *

Sara's body felt lighter than air. She was floating along in the river—no, the air—and bumping against small clouds along the way. She could feel herself being lifted by the wind and carried on the breeze around the farm. She could feel the warmth that undoubtedly was the sunshine, drawing her nearer and nearer to its fiery sphere.

She needed to take a deep breath but couldn't make her lungs inhale. What was wrong with her?, she wondered without any sense of panic. Why couldn't she seem to wake up and function like she normally would be able to? Was she drugged by some gangster, or had she been hit by a monster-sized beast?

Her thoughts were so confused. How was she supposed to think clearly when she couldn't seem to think at all? She thought of the water bill and wondered if it had been paid. That must be the reason there was no water for a drink. And she was so thirsty.

Her mind floated to the horses and whether they had been fed. They would need water too. Maybe she could drink some of theirs. Why wasn't there a bottle of water around the house to drink? She always kept water in the pantry.

She wanted her limbs to move towards the kitchen for a glass, but her legs and arms refused the motion. She must be in a deep, deep sleep to feel so sluggish and out of reality. Where was Ashton? Or was his name Houston? She couldn't quite seem to remember.

Where was William? He normally was around the house at this time of the day. He had often told her he watched over her when she slept, so why wasn't he here now to wake her? Had Lem or Ross or Marian or…Wait a minute! There was her father up ahead!

She hadn't seen him in a long time. Where had he been? Why was he here at Elizabeth's Place? And was that Mom with him?

A dark cloud blocked her view of the long hallway, and Sara's world tipped once again into the darkness. The dreams all stopped, and the floating in the air seemed to come to a halt. She didn't drop from the air or sink in the river where she floated. She simply froze in midthought and stopped. There was nothing more.

* * *

'There's her truck!' Ashton called to Ross as he yelled inside the cab of his truck. Lem and Herb sat in the front seat, but Ashton had insisted on standing against the back window in the bed of the truck. That way, he determined, he could see her on the horizon.

'Where, boy? Where do you see her truck?' asked Herb in a panic.

'There, to the left of the pole,' answered Ashton. 'Pull over here, Lem, in this gravel spot. Her truck is down in the gully there, past the fence line.'

Before the truck had come to a complete stop, Ashton leapt from the bed to the rocky ground that bore the skid marks of Sara's tyres. Hours ago she had left the house for the store. According to Marian and the old boys, she had left them with eggs and pie shells some time ago as well. So according to the calculations of Lem and Ross, she had to be between the house and the store, but not on the regular road that Ashton had walked to find her.

That was when Herb suggested the old Ebbington Road. Not many folks used it anymore as it only connected two farms to the main highway. Old Man Ebbington, for whom the road was named, had died more than twenty years ago, and his farm sat empty having been inherited by some nephew someplace up north. Emmett lived down the road on a small farm that he used for cattle and an occasional garden. That only left Amos Loyd, who was a little deafer than deaf and a whole lot more cantankerous than the average sleeping-but-now-awakened bear! Loyd had once been a great strawberry farmer, but his back gave out, and his manners had never been so good to begin with, so the patch had grown over, and the eager strawberry pickers that once visited were gone.

It was his bulls that had been fighting, even though, to Herb's way of studyin' it, they could have done that right at home. Instead they had chosen throughout the last few months to wander the roadside, as if seeing the sights, and when they came to a likely place, having a knock-down-drag-out between themselves for entertainment. The only problem was that anyone in their way when the time came for the wrestling match was bound to get caught in the middle. He had to wonder if that was what had happened to Sara, her pie shells, and the truck.

'Take it easy when you start down this incline, Herb,' Ashton ordered, holding out a hand to help the man down the bank.

'I've been walking longer than you've known how to chew and whistle!' came his ornery reply as the three men limped and slid to the bottom of the steep hill. 'Don't be thinking just because you're younger'n me that you can boss me around, ya hear?'

Ashton understood the command explicitly and, ignoring them, hurried to the truck sitting catawampus in the field. The mucky mud was squishy and gooey as Ashton's feet sunk into the murky mess. The wheels of the truck looked like they had experienced a similar sensation as the black stuff lined over the rim of the tyres in most incidents.

Ashton peered into the truck window and saw Sara, head against the steering wheel and arm crookedly hanging against the window handle. She didn't move, and Ashton was afraid to open the door himself because he might add injury to the insult of wrecking her truck.

Herb made it to the truck, out of breath but still in one piece. 'Looks like she'll be needin' more eggs before she cooks anythin',' he said as he traced the fragments of eggshells and yolk that had run down the driver's window. 'Bet the pie crusts are broken in too many pieces to bake too.'

Ross put his hand on Ashton's shoulder and looked inside the cab. 'Do you want to open the door on the other side, and she is she, um, you know…?' he reasonably questioned. 'If she ain't, guess we should try to get her out?'

'No, we can't take her out, not without someone trained in that kind of thing,' Ashton replied with more than a bit of worry in his tone. 'I will go to the other side and see if the door will open. Then I'll try to reach her and check her pulse.'

'Well, don't just try, confound it! Do it, boy! Get at it!' Lem hollered at him. 'Time's a-wastin'!'

Knowing the man was right, Ashton tried to hurry to the passenger-side door. However, the effort was like swimming in quicksand, and at one point, he thought he had lost a shoe, if not two. He finally reached the other door, sitting even deeper in mud, and wrestled with the door handle.

'It's locked! Why in the world does a girl who can get in more trouble than a politician on election day lock the dad-burned doors on the way to the house?' Ashton bellowed to the sky. 'Of all the silly—'

'Boy, break out the window!' Herb demanded. 'What's a little window that's shattered after all the rest of the damage she's done? Break out the window!'

Reaching into the bed of the pickup, Ashton tried to locate something to smash the window with as he continued to fight for his balance with the mud sucking at his heels. Finally he found a crowbar, and climbing up the wheels and side of the truck, he managed to get his hand around it and pull it to himself.

He pretended to take a step backwards but instead just raised the iron bar and swung it like a batter headed for a homer. The window cracked into a million pieces, but the safety woven throughout the window stayed in one continuous piece of broken fragments.

He pushed inward with the bar to make a hole big enough for his arm to reach through and then raised the push-down button on the side of the door, releasing the locking mechanism and allowing the door to open.

The heat inside the truck was thick when he managed to open the door from the frame with a *re-c-h-i-n-g* sound as metal scraped against metal. He kicked his feet as he leaned his knees against the opening so that the mud would release them, and slowly, he was able to climb inside the cab of the truck.

'Well, what are you waitin' for? Check on her already!' Lem screamed at Ashton, his patience losing a battle with anxiety.

Ashton scooted across the seat, reaching for Sara and worrying what she would say if she could see the mud now piling in mounds on her floorboard and bench seat. He touched the temple of her head and wiped at the blood already drying on her cheek. Though it was weak, he thought he felt a pulse. Just to be sure, he took her wrist in his right hand and felt along the side of her arm.

'We have a pulse!' he said excitedly to the men outside the truck. He leaned over Sara and unrolled the window as best he could and handed his cell phone out to the older men. 'Call 911,' he ordered, 'and tell them where we are.'

'That's twenty or more miles away, Ashton,' said Lem. 'Couldn't ya just get her out yourself?'

'You mean there are no emergency personnel in the area? How can this be possible in the twenty-first century? What kind of hick town do you people live in?'

Lem, Herb, and Ross all looked at each other in exasperation.

'We happen to live in the best town around, buddy, and if you can't do something to help this little girl, we'll call Doc Lynn and get him over here,' Herb hollered back at an astonished Ashton.

'And who is Doc Lynn?' asked Ashton.

Ross looked at Lem, and together they both looked at Herb.

Calmly, Ross spoke. 'Doc Lynn is the veterinarian in these parts, Ashton. He can sew up a hand or bandage ya up in a jiffy. He's been retired several years, which is why he moved to this neck of the woods so he won't be none too busy to help us.'

'Then call him! Call someone before she bleeds to death while you all stand there and watch!' Ashton had lost his cool while he looked at a very pale Sara. 'I can't believe there is no emergency help! What if one of you had a heart attack or something? Huh? What would you do then?'

'Guess we'd have to ride over to Gladesville or somethin',' answered Ross while Lem and Herb fussed with each other over the doctor's phone number.

Herb held the phone to his ear, but before Ashton could feel any relief at the situation, Herb said, 'How do you make this thing work? There ain't no dial tone on it.'

Ross smacked at his dentures and whistled that he knew how to dial the phone, so he took it from Herb and punched in the numbers before hitting

Send. Moments passed while the phone rang, and then finally a voice answered on the other end.

'Doc Lynn? This is Ross, and I'm over here at the Ebbington Road.'

Ross was silent as he listened and then responded a time or two with a 'yep' before telling the doctor that he was needed right away for an emergency. Ashton couldn't help but think that the conversation sounded anything but emergency-like and was about to explode with impatience when Ross clicked the End button on the phone and smiled through the window at him.

'Doc said he be here right away. He's over at Emmett's looking about a part for his tractor, so he'll be here in a sec.'

The final word ended with a whistle, and on any other day, Ashton would probably have cracked a smile, but as it was, the only thing he wanted to crack was Ross's head or at least his whistling teeth!

Hours seemed to pass before an old silver truck rumbled up the road.

'Hey! Over here!' Herb screamed towards the truck, waving his arm frantically at the same time. The motion almost made the man lose his balance, but his feet were, after all, firmly cemented in the thick mud of the field.

Ross and Lem joined in, and the truck pulled to the side of the road where a short man with white hair and broad shoulders climbed from the cab. The lack of urgency in his movement was about to kill Ashton, but, he thought, at least a man of medical training was on his way. How long it would take him to walk the distance or what he would know about the medical need once he reached them, he couldn't know. He patted Sara's hand as if to reassure her, if not himself, at the predicament in which they seeming to be drowning.

Faster than Ashton would have thought possible, Doc Lynn was at the truck door and asking him to gently hold Sara so that she didn't fall from the truck. The man immediately called the hospital in Gladesville and had an ambulance dispatched 'post-haste' to the site.

Efficient beyond Ashton's imagination, Dr. Lynn quickly bandaged Sara's head and checked her bones for any breaks. 'She took quite a lick to the head,' he pronounced. 'Her pupils are not responding, and her pulse is weak. Hi. I'm Dr. Mic Lynn. You are?'

Ashton completed the introductions and asked how long the ambulance would take. Dr. Lynn patted him on the shoulder and told him not to worry. They would arrive when they got there.

And finally, much to Ashton's relief, sirens could be heard in the distance. Due to the old road and its condition, it took the paramedics longer than usual to get to the accident site. By the time they arrived, a small train of onlookers trailed them. All lined up along the road to watch the action with several men self-proclaimed as traffic directors, should there be any vehicles to route around the scene.

While waiting, Herb had insisted that Ross dial the store and let Marian know what was happening.

He figured that would put her mind at ease knowing that Sara had been found and that it would give her plenty of gossip for the next few hours on the phone as she spread the word of the event.

Once the paramedics had checked the bandage around Sara's head, taken her vital signs, and checked her eyes for dilation or response, they bundled her up onto a gurney and hauled her, literally, through the pasture and up the hill to the awaiting ambulance. Ashton and Dr. Lynn both wanted to ride with her in the back, but Dr. Lynn was promoted to the front of the truck to ride with the driver.

Herb, Lem, and Ross made the executive decision to follow the ambulance because Ross would finally get to see what his new truck could do in an emergency situation. With the assistance of several onlookers, all the men help the three elderly and muddy men into the cab of the truck and directed them in backing and turning it around.

The thrill of another adventure began.

Chapter 18

His world was falling apart! First, he couldn't find Sara, and then when he did, he thought her dead. She was alive though, he kept reminding himself as he paced outside the parlour doors where he had placed her on the settee.

Houston wanted to put a fist through the wall to relieve his anxiety, but he knew that would be more harm than good, both to his fist and William's wall. A door somewhere in the house closed, and he jerked his head up to look in the direction of the sound. Unfortunately, it wasn't from the parlour, so he crept into William's study and sat in the dark recesses of the room.

He understood the peace that Sara said she felt here. Surrounded by books and rich colours, the room enveloped him in a comfortable cocoon as he chose a chair and sank into it. He leaned his head back against the comfortable leather and closed his eyes.

William entered the room and quietly took a seat across the room from him. He said nothing but gave Houston both the room to rest and the peace to heal, if only briefly. As he sat, he thought of all the antics that Sara had pulled in her life, some funny and memorable, others scary and debilitating. This one fell into the latter category, by far worse than any she had encountered thus far.

Tears filled his eyes and silently coursed down his cheek. She was so dear to his heart, like a child in many ways but a lady of grace in so many others. He felt like he had a deeper connection to Sara than he did with Houston, and he had known him a lifetime.

Houston stirred in the chair, and William looked in his direction. How did he offer comfort to Houston when he felt the need of comfort himself? And Elizabeth? How would he be able to help her heal from this tragedy?

The questions buzzed around in his head, banging into each other before garnering an answer. The doctor had finally arrived, but he feared it was too late for Sara. She was too cold and still for life to be a certain thing.

The door opened, and Cook came in, offering a pot of tea and some cookies for the men. Houston never opened his eyes; William took the tray from the woman whose eyes were filled with unshed tears. As he set the tray down on the table, he took Cook's hands and squeezed them in reassurance. She merely nodded her head and left the room.

Time was passing much too slowly this day. Answers weren't coming quickly enough, but he knew of no way to make them come faster. He paced the room and wished that, like Houston, he could slip away in restful sleep.

* * *

Hours passed slowly in a hospital. No matter how much coffee was consumed or how many times the men wandered to the restrooms, the day lingered for far longer than it normally would. Lem, Ross, and Herb took turns pacing the hallway. Ashton flipped through one magazine after another, rarely seeing the pictures printed on the pages and never reading a word.

Nurses went about their daily routine, checking on patients and changing shifts, but the four men in the waiting room remained stoic in their vigil. Only once did a doctor stop by to share news with them. As her only 'family,' any report would have come to them first.

Ashton had found emergency information in the desk at Elizabeth's Place. He had checked in several drawers, packed-away purses, and even her coat before he found the information he sought.

Sara was allergic to penicillin and sulfa drugs, information that was a necessity to the doctors. He had immediately relayed this to the hospital staff, and they quickly went to work on procedures to save her life. The initial consultation noted a possible broken rib or two, a dislocated shoulder, cracked collarbone, and bruised sternum. There was a chance that her spleen would have to be removed and that her wrist was broken. And that was just for starters.

How one girl could do so much damage was incredible to Ashton. She didn't even flip the truck! Of course, flipping would have been difficult because of the depth of the mud, so the truck appeared to slide across the field rather than bounce and roll. So how did she get so banged up?

Obviously that was an answer he wasn't going to get anytime soon, but in his mind, he could see her reaching for the groceries and simply running off the road, hitting the fence, bouncing into the ditch, and then flying through the air into the middle of the field, where the truck sank into the thawing pasture.

In this instance, he could see her walking away from the vehicle without a scratch. Well, maybe a bump on the head, but she could have walked away with very little wrong with her. Since that wasn't the case, what had happened?

Somewhere down the hall, beeps and dings were announcing an alarm. Two nurses walked quickly down to the room to discover the cause. An elderly man shuffled his way to a room to the left, and the elevator's bell announced the floor over and over. Still there was no word of Sara's condition.

Just before eight, Marian joined the group, having closed the store. She brought the men sandwiches and drinks so that they didn't have to leave the waiting room, but no one had much of an appetite. They opened a bag of chips and passed it around to share.

The hiss of a carbonated drink being opened broke the silence on more than one instance, but otherwise, the room was quiet.

Ross's head drooped, and a faint snore rose from Lem's bent head. Herb couldn't sit still long enough to drift off to sleep. He and Ashton played cards, swapped magazines, and even kept track of the colour of scrubs the nurses wore. Finally, just before eleven, a tall man in light blue scrubs rounded the corner and asked if they were the family of Sara McKenzie.

Eagerly, they nodded yes and rose to meet him.

'I am Dr. Neil Green,' the wiry man said. 'I want you to know that everything that can be done for Ms McKenzie is being tried. She is stable but remains unconscious, even though her MRI and other tests appear to be normal.

'There doesn't seem to be abnormal swelling in the brain, but she doesn't respond to anything we have tried. The surgical team has set the wrist and wrapped her ribs. Her spleen was removed due to the damage. We will be moving her to ICU when she comes from recovery. She is on a respirator as a precaution at this time, and we will continue to monitor all of her vital signs throughout the night.

'I wish I could tell you more good news, but frankly, we are at a wait-and-see stance now. There is really little that can be done until we see some response.'

Faces looking at him were lined with worry that he wished he could remove. There really was no medical reason why this young woman was in such critical condition, but she was. He answered their questions about when they could see her or if she would recuperate, even though he really didn't know the answers to many of them.

When he walked away, he was confident he had done all he possible could. He planned to check back on her as soon as he saw another patient, and he pushed the button of the elevator, knowing that the night ahead would be a long one.

'Well, what do you think, boys?' Lem asked as he swiped his hand across his face. 'Since we can't see her until morning, do you want to go home or stay here for the night?'

Marian answered for all of them with the authority only a mom can show in times of stress. 'You'll go home and get some rest. Sara wouldn't want you to sit here in a waiting room when comfortable beds are waiting at home. Get your stuff together, and I'll take you home. Ashton, what do you want to do?'

Without thinking, he said, 'I'll stay here and wait for her. If there are any changes, I will call you to let you know. I promise.'

Herb complained, and Ross agreed to leave his truck for Ashton. He dug his keys from his pocket, although Ashton assured them he wouldn't be driving anywhere. Still the keys were placed on the table, and Marian gave him a hearty hug before ushering the others to the elevator. As they waited for their ride to reach the floor, Marian turned and watched as Ashton hung his head in despair. It was then that she knew that his feelings for Sara were real.

* * *

Herb walked into his dark house and pulled off his jacket. Instead of heading to bed, he sat on the couch and unlaced his shoes before stretching out and pulling the throw over him. He had grown so attached to Sara in the short time she'd been in his life that he couldn't imagine a day without her smiling face.

She was a good girl, he thought, remembering the many ways that she had brought sunshine to his life—to all of their lives. From her cooking mishaps to her colourful knitting creations, Sara was always making things for the men.

Herb sat up on the couch and bowed his head.

'Lord, I know you can hear me, and even though I don't talk to you enough, I'm ready to talk now. I need your help. Please take care of Sara and heal her, Lord. She needs you right now, and I do too. Keep her safe, God. Bring her back to us who love her.'

Then, feeling that the problem was no longer his to handle, he lay down on the couch and fell asleep.

* * *

Elizabeth knocked gently on the door of the library. William was startled from his brief nap, and Houston jumped to his feet at the sound.

'The doctor has gone,' she said as tears raced down her cheeks. 'Sara has been tucked into her bed, but he seems very concerned for her.'

William took her in his arms and held her closely while she cried. He too wept silently with his wife as grief overtook the couple. Houston, upon hearing the news, raced to Sara's room, a place he had never visited, and sat by her bed.

As he watched her sleep, he said words of encouragement to her. He stroked her hair and held her hand. He memorised the way her breath sounded as she breathed in and out and the beauty that was so evident in her quiet slumber. He willed her dark lashes to lift from her cheeks and open those eyes that had held such mischief and life.

He touched her pale lips and urged them to laugh, to sing, to talk endlessly about silly things. Somewhere in the night, he leaned his head against the bed and dozed. He dreamed he felt her reach for him and touch his hair. But as he fitfully dozed in the chair, Sara's breathing became laboured and her skin cold.

Her gasping for air awakened him, and as she struggled to breath, he held her to him and told her of his love for her. As if hearing his testament, Sara's struggles ceased, and she was still. With tears pouring from his eyes, Houston gently kissed the woman that was to have been his bride and said his goodbyes.

His Sara was gone, and his heart was broken.

Chapter 19

Ashton walked to the nurses' station on the ICU ward and cleared his throat to gain attention from the nurse vigorously working at her desk.

'Yes? How can I help you?' the woman with the blonde ponytail and bright blue eyes asked Ashton as she turned to him and stared.

'Sorry to bother you, but could you tell me about the condition of Sara McKenzie? She was admitted to your unit late last night.'

'I am aware of my patients, sir. Ms McKenzie is still on a ventilator and still nonresponsive. The doctor isn't to visit for several minutes, but'—she glanced at the clock—'you can sit with her for ten minutes in exactly two hours if you'd like to have a seat in the waiting room.'

She turned her back and again began her paperwork, having both dismissed and apparently forgotten Ashton's presence.

'Humph,' he said impatiently. 'Could you tell me what is being done for her?'

Impatiently, she turned in her chair and crossed her arms over her chest. Glaring at Ashton, she reached for the clipboard that held patients' information and glanced over the notes listed there. 'According to the chart, Ms McKenzie was given one unit of—'

'I don't want to know what she was given,' Ashton interrupted. 'I simply wanted to know if she had been given pain medication or if the doctor had discovered what might be causing the unconscious condition.'

'According to the chart,' the brisk woman began again, 'there is no notation of what the cause of Ms McKenzie's condition is, nor is there any pain medication noted. Will there be anything else?'

'No, thank you. I think that just about wraps it up!'

'Good. Now, if you'll excuse me…'

Dismissed again, Ashton turned from the desk. He walked to the large windows that looked out on a world of white. It had snowed again early this morning, a cold blanket covering an even colder world.

He exhaled deeply and wrapped his coat closer to him. He was wrinkled from his overnight stay, but none the worse for wear. His wished he'd had a warmer sweater on as he sat in the lonely room. He'd only had on a T-shirt when he'd begun his search for Sara yesterday in the sunshine. Even then, he could have used a sweatshirt or thicker jacket, but his adrenaline had kept him warm in the ensuing hours.

Time ticked by as the two hours until he could see Sara crawled slowly. Ashton went in search of coffee and soon found a waiting room on another floor that offered pastries, coffee, and hot tea. The nurses there offered great hospitality, asking him why he was visiting and if they could do anything to assist him. The shorter more petite of the two batted her eyes at him more than once during their conversation. He wanted to ask her if she had something in her eye or if she was bothered by allergies, but because she had been so polite, he refrained.

When the clock showed the two hours had nearly completed their journey, Ashton rode the elevator back to the ICU floor and disembarked. He found the waiting room filled with anxious faces of family members of the patients on the ward and selected a seat closest to the nurses' station so as to not miss a single minute of visitation time with Sara.

A tall dark-haired male nurse read names of signed-in visitors and directed them down the hospital corridor to the appropriate rooms. His name was soon called, and he was shown to a glass-enclosed room where a tiny Sara lay covered with white sheets and blankets. Tubes seemed to be attached all over her small body as machines beeped and blinked to the side of the metal bed. White tape held a plastic tube to her mouth, offering her oxygen while she silently rested, perfectly still.

Ashton wanted to take her hand and hold it, but since he had never done so when she was awake and she could yell at him, he didn't dare to do it now.

He brushed the hair away from her eyes and saw the large purple bruise that had formed a nice-size goose egg on her forehead. Was that what was causing her lack of response? he wondered.

He leaned close and spoke to her, telling her about the new fallen snow. He suggested that she open her eyes so that she could make a snowman, but her eyelashes never moved. He tweaked her on the nose and told her they were all rooting for her recovery. Ashton mentioned Herb, Ross, Lem, and Marian and told her how they had all waited last night to hear from the doctor before heading home.

Too quickly the minutes flew by, and the nurse announced that all visitors had to leave the rooms. Ashton squeezed Sara's hand and told her to get well quickly as he also promised that he would be back to see her soon.

Though there had been no response to his words, Ashton felt certain that she had heard him and that she was encouraged by his visit. At least he was encouraged by seeing her, so he had to think that she would feel the same way.

Feeling slightly hopeful, he pushed the elevator button and waited for it to arrive. While he waited, he double-checked the visitation hours. Suddenly, beeping was heard in loud volume, and nurses ran down the hall in the direction of Sara's room.

Looking towards the room, he hurriedly turned and walked as fast as he dared in their footsteps, praying each step of the way that Sara was going to be okay.

* * *

Houston continued to hold Sara for long minutes after the life was gone from her body. William and Elizabeth entered the room and took in the suffering, clinging to each other in the act. Elizabeth encouraged Houston and William to leave the room so that Sara could be readied for burial, then turned and fled from the room, leaving Grace in charge of the preparations.

The day passed slowly as even Cook spent the hours crying at the loss of the young woman. Houston was bereft, knowing not what to do with himself as he awaited the undertaker to arrive at Elizabeth's Place. What had happened to her perfect life in such a short time?

William spent time in the library, a place he felt close to Sara. Elizabeth read sonnets and poems from books scattered in Sara's room while Grace chose Sara's favourite dress and placed the teddy bear Houston had given her for Christmas with her body.

Arrangements were made for her funeral and friends notified. Food was cooked to tempt the visitors offering condolences, but the reality of their loss was so foreign to the household that few stayed for any length of time. It was truly a house in mourning.

Draped in black, the clocks and mirrors were covered. The household was very quiet, and even the hounds sensed the loss. Events were cancelled, and William refused to discuss politics or his run for the Senate as the days grew longer. Time seemed to stop for all those involved at Elizabeth's Place.

Houston spent more and more time at his house, avoiding those he held dear and resisting the desire to sit by Sara's graveside. He began working passionately on the farm, clearing additional pastures and fields to expand his horse and crop production. If he smiled, it was a sight that few saw as the months passed by, and only he witnessed his unbearable pain.

With the passing of spring and the arrival of summer's bright sun, Houston gathered with William at the Capitol to rehash issues that had been left unfinished during the previous year's session of state Congress. Houston's grief turned into passionate rhetoric, opening avenues for his election to the State House just as William celebrated his election to the Senate.

Elizabeth gave birth to a beautiful baby girl in June, just as the honeysuckle bloomed with sweet blossoms. William beamed with pride at his newest joy, and the child was christened Sara Elise Cooper.

Houston attended the christening of little Elise and held her closely as he accepted his position of godfather in her life. He pledged to love and protect her always and contented himself in the years to come by basking in her antics and mischief that often rivaled his own sweet Sara.

Though he never married, Houston spent many a happy day at Elizabeth's Place visiting the family. He was as close a friend to William and Elizabeth as could be found and stood as a godfather to all four of the Cooper children.

On his deathbed, Houston, then in his eighties, still spoke of his love for Sara. He encouraged Elise and her brothers and sisters to never stop loving with their whole heart, just the way he had loved Sara and the way that William had always loved their mother, Elizabeth.

Houston was buried in the family cemetery on the acres of Elizabeth's Place beside his beloved Sara at the insistence of Elise, who cherished their love story. William placed a marble bench at the foot of the graves that would survive the generations of Coopers to come. Elizabeth, even though aged, grafted roses of bright red and white to be planted alongside the graves. It was a place of great beauty and sought after in the years to come by those desiring peace.

Chapter 20

Chaos ensued as Ashton stepped near the door of Sara's glass room. He watched without entering as they changed tubes, inserted needles, and turned knobs on the various machinery. In a whirlwind of motion, doctors and nurses arrived and left, each contributing something to the effort of keeping her alive.

The worst part of the whole scenario was the frustration of not knowing the actual cause of the crisis. A small bump on the head or a couple of broken bones should not be life-threatening to Ashton's way of thinking.

Over the next hour, doctors he'd not seen the previous night arrived to offer consultations. New medicines were put into use, and even a new monitoring device was installed.

An unexpected arm around Ashton caused him to jerk as Dr. Lynn, veterinarian turned life-saving pro, came to the floor to visit his almost-patient.

'She'll pull through,' the man said as he watched the various techniques working together. 'She seems to be a pretty tough cookie, and her brain isn't experiencing any swelling. Therefore, I'd say she'll suddenly perk up in the next day or so, and voila! Just wait and see!'

While Ashton wanted to trust the instincts of the man, he still had his doubts that the anatomy of a horse could provide the absolute details of a human's problems. However, he allowed himself to be led by Dr. Lynn, who spoke with nurses and doctors alike with great authority and knowledge, to the waiting room, where he sat in a seat that he deemed should bear his name.

'According to Dr. Mitchell, over in the dark blue scrubs, she was having difficulty breathing earlier. But he described it more like a panic attack reaction rather than a pulmonary problem. They have increased her oxygen so that her count will increase, and she will relax somewhat. There was no need to perform a trachea, so all is well, even though a lot of bodies and a bunch of beeping machines seem to say otherwise.'

Relieved that Dr. Lynn could speak medical jargon with ease, Ashton leaned into the chair and reclined his head. He sat that way for so long his neck was stiff when Dr. Lynn announced visiting hours were once again upon them. Ashton asked at the desk if Sara could have visitors and was allowed to see her for the appointed ten-minute span.

He talked openly with her as he sat next to her bed. He told her he was angry at her for not responding more quickly and that he was ready for a nap, so she needed to wake up and allow him to take one.

Ashton expected her temper to flare as he spoke, but instead, the steady in and out of the ventilator was his only response. He rubbed her shoulder and held her hands while he talked, hoping that the stimulation of touch would activate her mind and bring her out of the coma. When the time was up, Ashton leaned over and kissed her cheek. He promised her he would return and told her to mind her manners and listen to the doctors.

A bit happier than when he had entered, he left her room and returned to the waiting room, expecting to find Dr. Lynn still there. Instead, a quick whistle from the elevator drew his attention, and Dr. Lynn stood forcing the carriage door open until he arrived.

'So, did she listen to your every word?' the man asked as he punched the button for the ground level. 'She didn't hit you or anything, did she?'

With a chuckle, Ashton shook his head no and remained quiet the rest of the ride down the shaft. As the doors opened, bright sunshine flooded into the interior, immediately providing the energy his tired body needed to make the ride back to Elizabeth's Place.

'Want something to eat?' questioned Dr. Lynn, to which he nodded yes and headed out the front doors of the hospital.

'So, what sounds good to you?' Ashton asked as they crossed the parking lot. The older man gave him several suggestions and opened the truck door. The remainder of the afternoon was spent in conversation, discussing everything from atoms to zucchini, to turtles and sea squash.

By the time the sun began to set, Ashton had delivered the vet back to his truck, returned to Elizabeth's Place for a shower and change of clothes, and returned to the hospital. Though the visit had been low-key with Dr. Lynn, and while Ashton was more than inclined to enjoy the man's company, what he really needed was sleep.

He glanced at the clock as he entered the waiting room, signed into the visitor's log, and took his normal seat to wait. With only minutes to go, he relaxed into the soft leather of the chair and closed his eyes. Within seconds, he was sound asleep.

The minutes ticked by as visitors silently crept by Ashton. Their visits concluded, most left for the day, but others joined Ashton in sleep, spreading small jackets across their legs for comfort. Nursing shifts changed, and still he slept. One nurse, the friendly dark-headed one from the previous night, placed a blanket over him. Another brought him a cup of ice water for when he woke. Even the disagreeable nurse who was in charge of the station looked upon him kindly as he twisted and turned in his sleep to gain a better seat.

When the final visitation of the night was just moments from approaching, it was this nurse who gently shook him to gain his attention. He startled awake and looked at her in confusion before she told him he could enter Sara's room.

Staggering with unspent sleep, he stopped outside her door and watched her chest move up and down under the sheets. He spent his time sitting quietly with her, rubbing her arms and moving her hands in his own. He rose to leave, knowing time had once again expired, and he once again leaned over the bed. Just as he neared her face to kiss her cheek, one eyelid opened and stared at him.

So excited was he to see this that he ran screaming with emotion from the room. He grabbed the attention of the nurse and, holding onto her arm, pulled her back into Sara's room. The eye was still open and staring, to which the nurse said it was probably just a muscle spasm, but she checked her vitals.

She picked up the phone at the side of the bed and called for help. One nurse moved a machine into the room while the other took Ashton's arm and moved him out of way. He stayed as close as he could to watch the activities and keep his eye on Sara. Nurses exercised her arms and legs for responsiveness while another pulled her other eye open and checked it with a penlight.

Seeming pleased with the results, the friendly nurse turned and gave him a thumbs up and then waved him farther back as doctors responded to pages and tubes were removed from Sara's body. Because the room was getting rather full of people, Ashton slipped outside and watched from the window until someone pulled the curtain, blocking his view completely.

Pleased beyond belief but frustrated at not knowing what was presently taking place, he remained in the hallway until an aide took him by the arm and handed him a cup of coffee.

'The doctors are pleased with her progress, so perhaps now would be a good time for you to get some sleep,' she said, escorting him down the hall. 'I will call you if anything changes. Do we have your number on record?'

Ashton hastily wrote his name and number on a pad of ordinary white paper and handed it back to the pretty aide. He muttered a thanks as she took it and stuffed it into her apron's front pocket, then Ashton made his way one more time to the elevator.

Days passed in much the same way. While Sara was improved and breathing on her own without the help of the ventilator, she was not moved from the ICU room. Instead, she was watched closely as she responded to different levels of noise and stimulation. She was still in a comatose state, but she began to show reaction to certain things around her.

Once, while Herb was sitting with her, he touched her hand, and she returned his touch with a squeeze of his fingers. Marian was talking to her about strawberry pies that she had made the night before, and Sara burst out laughing, startling Marian. With Ashton, she would attempt to open her eyes, but because they didn't quite respond, her eyelids would wiggle with motion.

He took to reading to her just so she could hear his voice. He read the newspapers and the comics to her as well as a book that he found on her nightstand. He picked up where she had bookmarked but made certain that he kept the page's corner turned down so she would know where she had stopped her own reading.

Then one night as Ashton was saying goodbye to her, she lifted her hand and sought his. Her eyes never opened, nor did her eyelids do their wiggly dance, but she reached and held his hand. Tears streamed down his face as he placed his other hand on top of hers. It wasn't his imagination when he saw a smile caress her lips.

From that day forward, Sara grew stronger. Her eyes would open for long moments at a time, and she would reach for the hands of those who visited her. She still didn't speak or respond to words directed to her, but Marian swore that she was listening to all they said.

The day that Herb brought her fresh flowers to the windows outside her room, she actually responded with a broad smile. The blossoms weren't allowed in the room, but a nurse did bring a small table to hold them so that she could view them through the glass. As they all stood in the hallway, Ashton hurried into the room. She lifted her arm and extended it to welcome him. She flashed him a smile and laughed out loud at his surprise.

That night, they moved Sara to a private room and soon thereafter began a rigorous regime of physical therapy. The specialists worked with her speech development as well as instructing her in eating practices and slowly into walking. The first time she sat alone on the edge of the bed made Marian cry. When she motioned for water, it was Herb who handed her the glass and watched her raise it to her lips with pride.

By the time she was released from the hospital almost a month later, the grass was a vibrant green, and the trees were full of leaves. Sara had changed almost as much as nature surrounding her. She walked to the car on almost steady legs. She knew to lower her head to get into the vehicle, and she understood how to buckle the seat restraint.

Ashton drove her back to Elizabeth's Place in his rental car. Emmett had long ago finished with Red Belle, and though she ran, she also had a tendency to be temperamental. Not desiring a problem that might upset Sara, he opted to keep the rental he been using. He drove with caution, but Sara didn't seem to have any qualms about riding in a car.

As he turned into the gates of Elizabeth's Place, Sara's eyes darted left and right to take in the trees and flowers along the side of the drive. The roses were in bright bloom, as were the iris and the wisteria that was full of great purple blossoms.

The minute the house appeared before her, Sara gasped and broke out in a huge smile. She beamed at the house with a look of love. When the car stopped, she unbuckled the tricky belt with no problem. Opening the car door, she scooted out of the car and ran to the front porch, where she wrapped her arms around the posts with enthusiasm.

Sara had journeyed through miles of recovery and even farther through lifetimes. But she was getting well now. Even more importantly, Sara was back at Elizabeth's Place, the place where her whole heart could heal. Once again, she was finally at home.

Chapter 21

William sat in the alcove of the library and watched her as she stumbled across the floor to the library. When she plopped into her favourite chair, he let out a breath he hadn't realised he was holding. She was finally at home, but she hadn't looked for him or even mentioned his name.

For Sara, the healing was just beginning. It was not just a physical healing, but largely an emotional one. Her mind was remembering things and events that she logically knew could not have happened to or with her. Yet it was vivid in her mind.

As she sat in the library, scenes ran through her mind of dances and elaborately decorated rooms at Elizabeth's Place. She heard voices of conversation that she couldn't have had, but she knew every word.

And she ached for the ones missing from her heart. How she longed to wrap her arms around Houston. But she didn't know anyone named Houston. Could she possibly be mistaking Ashton's name for Houston?

But she knew that she wasn't. She could sense him, and in certain rooms, she could smell his cologne and feel his presence. She had even turned yesterday to say something to him, looking at the seat in the parlour where she just knew he would be, but of course, he wasn't. And that was because he was only a figment of her imagination. Right?

She wandered slowly upstairs to her room but paused in front of the door that would lead to Elizabeth and William's room. She opened the heavy door, but only an unused bed and an empty wardrobe were in the room. The floor had recently been vacuumed for the lines left by the cleaner were still marked on the carpeting.

This was maddeningly confusing! She became so depressed and frustrated with the thoughts floating through her mind that she thought she was totally mad! She tried to discuss her confusion with Herb, but she stopped midway through because she sounded, even to her ears, like a patient at Bedlam.

Despite her growing strength and abundance of energy early in the mornings, she slept only briefly during the nights, often dreaming of riding in the pastures or searching for people she realistically knew she had never met. She stopped eating normal meals and rarely visited the stables anymore. Not only was it difficult to walk through the grass, she just didn't seem to have the will. She needed...She needed William!

As she sat in the library with the curtains drawn closed, it was perfectly quiet and peaceful. Except that in Sara's mind, there was little peace to be found. A sob caught in her throat as she agonised over her life and the turn it had taken. Where was rational thinking? Had a bump from the simple accident left her so inane?

She wept for long minutes, covering her face in her hands.

At the sound of her agony and the sight of her tears, William could stand his silence no longer. He came to her and, without startling her, took her in his arms and held her. It was like a part of her was immediately restored.

'Sara, I am so sorry for all you have endured,' William began. 'I need you to hear me and to understand what I am going to tell you. Do you know who I am?'

She glanced at him with eyes full of tears and heartbreak. 'Yes, I know you. You are the William I have come to know and love while I have been at Elizabeth's Place. But you are also the William I dream of, just as I dream of Elizabeth and Houston and Cook and so many others. William, I am losing my mind!'

As she gasped through her confusion and pain, he held her closely. He had so much to explain to her and even more that on faith she must believe in order to survive this roadblock in her life. He wanted to take away all the pain she held, but he knew that in order to overcome the misery she felt, she first had to accept the memories she thought of as imaginings.

He rocked her like a small child until the tears subsided. Holding her in his lap with his arms around her, William began his story.

'Elizabeth was an incredible woman, just as you are, Sara,' he began. 'What you know of her is fact. And you saved her from a terrible fate. Do you have any thoughts of such a thing?'

Sara was very still for long moments. Perhaps she was scraping her mind for events that made sense, or perhaps she was simply still, he didn't know. Yet she nodded her head in understanding and leaned closer to him.

'I remember a time when Elizabeth and you lived here at Elizabeth's Place. I lived here too,' said Sara in all but a mumble. 'I remember that I had an accident in the carriage, and Samuel found me and brought me back to the house, this house. I had a broken arm.'

William rubbed her back and waited until she finished.

'You are correct. You did those things, Sara. Not some dream or imagined happening, but an actual event. Why or how, I don't understand any better than you. But I do want you to completely believe that you did see, hear, and walk through that time period. I think it must have been because of the truck wreck you experienced, but however it happened, you walked with me and with Elizabeth daily.

'You knew Samuel, Houston, and the man we called Thomas. You experienced a great love with Houston and enjoyed dancing and merriment of a special Christmas. But most of all, you single-handedly changed fate, Sara!'

He took a deep breath, held it, and waited for her response. There was nothing from her except silence as she processed all he was telling her. She replayed his words over and over in her mind, reassured that his words were true and that she wasn't going mad with all the wanderings her mind produced.

She briefly lifted her head and looked into his eyes. 'Tell me more,' she whispered.

And he did. He told her of sleigh rides over the snow, of proposed academy buildings and Thomas's deceit. He told her of Elizabeth's sweet ways and the elaborate party that was held. He rocked her as he relayed Houston's proposal and Elizabeth's pregnancy. And then, he told her of her death in that century and reawakening in this one.

'But if Elizabeth didn't die that night, if she lived a long life and you had several children, why are you still here with me?'

He smiled sweetly down at her, wiping tears from her face.

'For such a time as this, sweet Sara,' he said, 'God allows His angels to have wonderful moments with those they love. I knew you would need me more here than anyone else could have ever needed me before. I am here to hold you and help you heal. You are wonderfully and delightfully made. Never fear that you are alone.

'You were willing to sacrifice yourself because of the love you hold for Elizabeth and for me. The least

I can do is help you understand the worlds you have lived in and the people you have loved.'

Sara took a deep breath and rested gently in his arms. There were many more questions she needed answers to, but for tonight, what she had just learned was enough to process. As he rocked her in his arms, she relaxed for the first time in many nights.

And there, she slept.

Chapter 22

Ashton noticed almost immediately the change that took place in Sara. The following morning, she was much more enthusiastic for life again and wore a smile on her face and a confident air she hadn't had in weeks. He walked with her to the barn to see the horses and feed the other critters that wandered through her doors. She basked in the warmth the animals gave her but seemed to tire much sooner than he had anticipated.

Once the feeding was complete, he scooped her in his arms, an act that she had never experienced with Ashton, and laughingly carried her back to the house. He made funny facial expressions and complained jokingly about her heavy weight as he placed her gently on the overstuffed chair in the sitting room. Here the morning sun flooded through the windows, and the birds chirping outside seemed a part of the room.

'I know I am slow, but I don't think I need to be carried around like a child. The next time you try that, I may have to bop your nose,' Sara announced with humour.

'Okay, well, with a threat like that, I am not sure I can take a chance of hauling you around again. Between the damage you could do to my nose and the weight of your huge body, I don't think carrying you will be worth the effort!'

'Oh, you brute!' she screamed as laughter pealed from her. 'How can you say such a horrid thing to me—a poor invalid—and still sleep at night!'

Ashton joined her in laughter and sat on the arm of the chair. As the merriment began to die down, he leaned over to kiss her but, in the last second, picked some straw from her hair instead. If Sara noticed his change of mind, she didn't mention it but rather told him that baking a pie sounded like a perfect endeavor for the afternoon.

'What type of pie do you want to bake? 'Cause I could eat dozens of pies if you are going to start spoiling me with baking,' Ashton said. 'You never did make that strawberry pie you promised.'

'Sorry,' she giggled, 'but I've been a little preoccupied of late. What is your favourite pie?'

He tousled her hair and lifted her chin as her head leaned back to look him in the eye.

'I think I would be really fond of "Sara" pie if I was ever offered that,' he replied softly, and he bent down and kissed her.

At first, Sara was so startled that she gasped in surprise, but when he continued, she began to respond. She enjoyed being kissed, and Ashton seemed very skilled at the art. When the kiss ended, he continued to hold her near. While she enjoyed the closeness, she also felt a bit wistful that William or Houston weren't the ones offering such affection. She toyed with this thought only briefly before giving into the feelings that were developing for Ashton.

Later that afternoon, Ashton sat with her in the library and read to her. His melodic voice soothed any uneasiness she might have indulged in if she was by herself, so she knew that spending time with Ashton was as therapeutic as the leg exercises he made her do. She promised herself to climb out of the funk she was in and only think of positive things.

Sara spent time late that night with William at her side, exploring the different avenues her mind wandered when she thought of the past weeks. He explained to her about Houston and his life after her departure as well as his happiness with the children William and Elizabeth brought to life.

For Sara, the past was sorting itself out into different chapters. She reflected on different events, but she was no longer dwelling on them in sorrow or regret. She was, piece by piece, putting that life in perspective and attempting to divide it from the life she now experienced.

William encouraged her to give her heart to Ashton and build a happy life at Elizabeth's Place. Only once did she ask him about his love for her. He explained that she was a little sister he had never been blessed with in his life. He wanted to see her happy, healthy, and safe and promised he would never leave her side.

Knowing that she was as spoiled as a newborn child, she languished in the love shown to her by both Ashton and William. But there were others who loved her as well, and in her mind, she had been neglecting them terribly.

The following morning, with Ashton leading the way, Sara made her way to the country store where Herb, Lem, and Ross welcomed her with open arms. Marian stood to the side until each of the gentlemen had finished their hugs, then she wrapped the frail girl in her arms like a mother hen. She was so glad to see Sara that she almost cried.

'It has been too long without you here, Sara,' she said. 'We have missed you!'

Sara glowed in their cheerful words and soon was seated around the table with them as the men shared stories of numerous things that occurred while she had been ill.

'I didn't think there were enough people in Crawdad for me to have missed so much,' she said as they picked on her. 'I can't believe anything happened, to be honest.'

'Well, with the exception of that fishing trip Ross took, nothing much did happen,' Herb admitted.

'Fishing trip? Do tell!' Sara said with a lifted eyebrow.

'What? You don't know about the fishing trip?' Ross asked. 'Why, it was the biggest—'

'Crock of malarkey anyone ever dreamed up,' Herb finished.

Lem barked with laughter, and Marian handed cookies all around that she had been baking when Sara and Ashton arrived.

The cinnamon smelled delicious. Taking a big bite, Sara realised that the apples and raisins in the cookie added both a delightful texture and flavour to the cookie. Marian said she had named it Sara's pie.

'But it's not a pie,' Sara began, but Herb interrupted her.

'Of course it's not a pie, but since we've known you, you've started to make about a jillion "pies," and you ain't made a one yet! So Marian took stuff that she would normally put in an apple pie—'

'And some other ingredients to give it a special flair—'

'And she made a cookie that we could all enjoy before starving to death waiting on yours!'

When all had finished the explanation, Ashton had eaten three of the cookies and pronounced them all delicious. Everyone around the table laughed at the abundance of cookies that were consumed as well as the relief they felt at having Sara back in their midst.

'Ashton, I forgot to ask you,' Sara said as the cookies were swapped for bottles of milk and water. 'What happened to your car? Did Emmett ever get it fixed?'

All eyes turned to Ashton, who tried at first to ignore them as he reached for the last cookie. But the silence drew on, and he knew he had to come clean about the vehicle's status.

'Well, to be honest, Red Belle is about as fixed as she will ever get. Emmett is a good repairman. I think he took the whole car apart, bit by bit, and then put her back together. But her running days are over. Oh, she might make it to the store or such, but there is no way for her to make the journey back to the West Coast.'

'So what are your plans, boy?' Herb asked.

'Well, I guess I could buy a new car and either travel farther east or north, or I could even just go back, but frankly, I don't feel that going back is an option much anymore.'

'Why's that?' Lem wanted to know. 'You lost your job or what?'

'I had quit my job long before I came to Crawdad, Lem,' he answered, 'but I don't think that the Coast is where I belong anymore. I feel like this is home now. So I guess I'll find a place to live and stay on around here, if ya'll will have me.'

He grinned up at Marian, who placed a hand on his shoulder. Herb 'hmmphed' at the announcement, and Ross and Lem remained silent.

'I don't know of any place around here close that has anything for rent,' Herb said, looking as though he was really studying on the idea. 'I bet you could get something closer to Gladesville though. They've got some apartment buildings there in the city.'

'I don't think I want to be in a city,' Ashton said, a bit disappointed, 'regardless of how small that city is. I would love to find a farm to live on and try my hand at farming.'

'Really? You, a farmer?' Ross asked. 'I got plenty of land for you to try before you buy and get in over your head.'

'I might just take you up on that, Ross.' Ashton sat closer to the man and began to ask questions about crop rotation and fertilisation techniques. The afternoon passed quickly as they all chatted about things of absolutely no importance.

As Sara and Ashton rose to leave and hugs had been given all around, Ashton promised to stop in to see Ross one day soon to discuss their farming partnership. Marian rolled her eyes in exasperation as the men once again started a discussion.

'Sara is tired and wants to go home, fellas,' Marian announced. 'Let that subject lie for a while and think it over. You can talk some more in a few days.'

That subject tucked away, however briefly, the two young people walked to the rental car and crawled inside.

'You know, you have to take this car back soon,' Sara insisted, and Ashton acknowledged her but didn't elaborate on the subject.

When they arrived back at Elizabeth's Place, just as Sara started to open the door, Ashton grabbed her wrist and held her back.

'I don't want to buy a car. I want to buy us a truck so that we can use it on the farm,' he said. 'I think a tractor might also be in the picture very soon. What do you think?'

'I thought Ross had a tractor to use,' Sara said. 'I asked him to borrow it once myself.'

'You aren't hearing me, Sara. I want *us* to have a farm *here* at Elizabeth's Place. I want us to have a tractor and a baler and some of the equipment that produces crops and helps us make a good living here.'

'Here? At Elizabeth's Place? Why, I had thought a garden in the spring was a lot to undertake, but—'

'But nothing! We can do this, Sara. We can make a wonderful farm life for our family. It will be hard work, and I know there will be times when we want to throw in the towel, but we can make it a successful place.'

Sara was listening, but all she heard was the word *family* before her eyes got big and her ears quit hearing his words.

'What?' she asked. 'What did you say, Ashton? Not about the crops or the planting, but the part about our family?'

'Yeah, a man's got to have a family to help on the farm. Herb and Lem and Ross won't be around forever to help me out, so I'll need some boys to be ready to pitch in to do the work.'

Sara just smiled. He must think that babies were born at the age of ten to be able to start plowing fields and milking cows! Mercy!

Ashton came around the car and opened her door, helping her out and into the front door. The house seemed to smile at the notion of children and laughter in the home again. There was promise and excitement in the air around them again.

Elizabeth's Place was indeed full of treasure, Sara thought. But that treasure wasn't necessarily hidden in her caves or groves that surrounded the house. Instead, the treasure was in the family that dwelt there.

Sara still believed there were many mysteries to uncover at Elizabeth's Place but that would save until another day.

As William watched from his favourite spot in the library, Ashton and Sara began mapping out their own design for happiness. He knew that just as Elizabeth's Place had blossomed with the energy and love he and Elizabeth had shared, Sara would ensure, with Ashton's help, that the love never left the beautiful home. For after all, home was where the heart was, and there was a bountiful supply of heart at Elizabeth's Place.

For now,

The End

CPSIA information can be obtained
at www.ICGtesting.com
Printed in the USA
FSHW021440071218
54252FS